NANDIA'S COPPER

Also by Ned Wolf

Awaken Your Power to Heal
Sailing on a Banshee Wind
Floraporna

NANDIA'S COPPER

BOOK I OF THE NANDIA TRILOGY

NED WOLF

THE THERAPEUTAE

PRESS

Published by:

The Therapeutae Press
P.O. Box 23542
Flagstaff, AZ
U.S.A. 86002

Paperback ISBN: 978-0-9675575-4-0
Ebook ISBN: 978-0-9675575-5-7

TheTherapeutaePress.com

THE THERAPEUTAE

PRESS

DEDICATION

… to all who follow the yearning to nurture
the growth of consciousness.

I

TELEPORTING INTO THE GREAT CHAMBER of the Galactic Council ended just as abruptly as it had begun. All motion stopped as the brilliant, spiraling, white light cleared from my head. I looked around, first at the unusual array of beings seated at a curved dais above me, then at the gloomy chamber that surrounded us. It looked as ancient as Agoragon, my mentor, had described it—fivescore or more centuries old, by his reckoning.

When he notified me of this journey, he hadn't prepared me for the sudden projection that had propelled me here. Another of his coyote-like teaching tricks, I decided. My no-spring-chicken of a teacher delighted in playing pranks, which did add spice to his invariably long and solemn sermons, to be sure. He would regularly remind me to hold my horses and focus on the present. "And the purpose of such equine equanimity is what, Bernard?" he would ask, his gaze resting steadily upon me as he awaited my response.

"The present is my only point of power." While trying to sound dutiful, I knew I sounded impatient.

I did have a tendency to impulsively dart off into the future, anxious to see what gifts, troubles or promises the present might bring. Taking a deep breath, my mind stilled. I remembered where I was. It suddenly became very clear to me that my horses definitely needed to be reined in.

This was my first meeting with the Grand Council. In response to an urgent summons a week earlier, Agoragon had submitted my bona fides as a delegate candidate. The memory rekindled old apprehensions, which I decidedly did not want to wrestle with at that moment. Instead, I let my mind wonder about the Council. Why had they chosen such a dark and gloomy place? The domed marble ceiling, deeply smudged, must have been cobwebbed from antiquity. A golden light emanated from God-knows-where, highlighting the Elders before me and the spot where I stood. The rest was shrouded in shades of grey and dark. After another long breath, I had to admit that I felt like a schoolboy being accosted by his angry headmaster. In short, I could not have been more apprehensive.

"This place effectively shields us from mental eavesdropping." This telepathic explanation seemed to have been timed to let me to clear my head. I scanned the Elders seated atop the semicircular dais, hoping to identify the message's source. It was a male voice I'd mentally heard, flavored in an accent unknown to me. However, since the raised Council table seated only two beings who were remotely female, the gender of the telepathic Elder did little to help me identify him.

Agoragon had briefly mentioned that the Council

was represented by a wide diversity of life forms. I could hear his irritating coyote chuckle as it dawned on me how unhinged I was becoming at the raw novelty of what I was seeing.

"We need today's decisions to be well hidden from telepathing intruders," the voice continued. "If these proceedings go as hoped, Bernard, we trust you are prepared to travel?"

"I am quite prepared t ..., t ..., to travel." I recoiled in apprehension as I heard the stammer in my voice. I had just violated my solemn oath to exude only confidence at this meeting. The growing wave of apprehension welled up through my body. And then I made matters worse by blurting out, "I hope no one here views me as food, do they?"

In the silence that followed, I vacillated between feeling ashamed of the blunder and feeling hopeful. Ashamed that, once again, I had failed to rein in my horses. Hopeful that the remark would be seen as a bit of lighthearted humor. And even more hopeful that it would deflect the Council's attention away from my fears.

"Feather-light humor, I will, perhaps, concede," replied an incredibly large, black, ugly creature. "To several of us, you do look and smell like a small, yet delectable, morsel. Your attempted joke reveals that you know of the famines of long-ago, when humans were a food source for several of our species. But our purpose today is not culinary.

"Your teacher, Agoragon, we hold in high regard. We trust him. For many years, he graced these chambers, quite generous with his wisdom. He would not have teleported you here were you not fully capable of

3

looking after your own well-being. I say this despite your question about our appetites. We fully expect that you can exercise your innate power to hold yourself above violation. And so ...," he paused. I worried, wondering what was coming next.

"... and so," he continued, "I imagine your question about our appetites was to determine just how well you've masked your insecurities?"

I nodded. I resumed breathing deeply. Then I decided to simply accept my feelings of trepidation and give up trying to control them. I remembered Agoragon's advice that my feelings of fear are cooperative messengers—feelings I can learn from provided I don't try to hide or fight them.

"I have long looked forward to this meeting," I focused my thoughts toward the entire Council. "Yes, I fully accept that I am creating my life and my state of well-being. And I hope that if you did want breakfast, I would serve something more satisfying than eggs Béarnaise." Several Council members chuckled appreciatively at the pun I had made of my name.

"I am honored that my training and talents have been honed enough to be granted this opportunity." My confidence grew, and I mentally telegraphed my gratitude. "I wish to follow only the highest ideals for my life. I dream of being a Council delegate. Yet, I must admit, that in my fervor to be of use, I have worried that my fears would somehow disqualify me."

I had accomplished much during my fifteen-plus years of training. Agoragon had helped me to fully accept the talents and abilities I had developed. "If you are hoping to project humility by minimizing or hiding your talents, you limit their growth," he had chided.

Once was enough for that message. That day, I learned that my false modesty was an attempt to prove that I was humble. Which was not the same as being humble. The Grand Council had long been recognized as supporting only the highest ideals for human endeavor, and here I was, in the midst of my greatest dream.

An ancient institution, the Council boasted no army, no police force, no power to impose economic sanctions upon a planet. Yet, it was well regarded for its accomplishments. Council Elders were chosen from only the most advanced societies, each individual well-known for their wisdom, intelligence and perspicacity. For uncounted centuries, the Council had aided civilizations that aspired to the exalted purpose of nurturing individual talents, abilities and purposes. It held to the ideal that each individual's greatest passion is to contribute to the evolution of consciousness. The Grand Council had long demonstrated that nurturing that ideal was the most effective means of building sustainable, creative societies.

By the time of my interview before the Council, only a handful of planets had evolved beyond the need for Council interventions to resolve wars, famines and epidemics. These planets were home to civilizations that had elevated social consciousness to the point where they no longer needed to create such suffering in order to grow.

However, most planets still held to the economies of avarice, guilt and fear. So they created extremes in abject poverty and obscene wealth. The best of these still had grossly ineffective health-care systems, war machines that devoured a lion's share of energy and resources, deteriorating environments and educational systems that preached mostly superstition and irrational thought. When such a society reached a crisis, the Grand Council sent in delegates to help remedy the situation. These delegates were healers of renown with a resilience beyond the human norm. Over the centuries, many delegates had failed in their missions. Some died. Some of the more troubled planets self-destructed. Some few evolved and instituted the contributions of the Grand Council and its delegates.

So, here I was at the very epicenter of the greatest dream for my life. Once again, I reminded myself to rein in my horses. Letting my consciousness reach out to the Council, I telepathically acknowledged my desire to openly and honestly reveal myself. I felt, at the very least, that they deserved that.

In return, they seemed to have a humorous, if somewhat sardonic attitude toward me. As I scanned the different Elders seated at the Council table, I was drawn to one of the women. An unusual beauty, she fit no description I'd ever known of a Council Elder. I felt embraced in a blanket of warmth and wondered if she was sending me an affectionate nudge. She appeared youngish, dressed in autumnal colors that picked up golden highlights in her otherwise auburn hair. But it was her almond-shaped eyes that captured my attention. As if cast from some rare, blue-green gemstone, they projected an intelligence that piqued my curiosity and calmed me at the same time. I reined in my excitement and recalled my last meeting with Agoragon.

We had wandered through his Zen gardens until he bade me sit beneath the wide canopy of a Banyan tree. There, he filled our cups with his predictably acrid-tasting tea. As we sipped, I complained of my impatience and frustration over the few opportunities I'd had to express my skills. He had simply smiled and reminded me that within all desire lay the keys to its fulfillment. Then, he had washed my feet. Now, that was a truly humbling experience.

My reverie was interrupted by the large, dark Elder who had spoken earlier. "He must have his uses, otherwise Agoragon would not have honored him so." This was directed to a rotund humanoid seated to his right, a smaller gentleman as hairless as a billiard ball. He was garbed in a glittering golden robe reminiscent of a Liberace gown.

My great-aunt Tilly was in love with Liberace. Even decades after his demise, he was regaled for his flamboyance, his pompadour and his masterful piano playing. During my childhood visits to Aunt Til, I was sternly urged to sit and watch vids of his performances on an ancient black-and-white television.

With a piercing look, the bald Elder spoke. "Recommend your abilities to us, please, Bernard."

"While you're well aware that I can be notoriously clumsy in social situations," I began, "I am quite effective in helping people heal. And, I'm a fair hand at using my thoughts to seed my desired outcomes. I'm also known for my skill at extricating myself from sticky situations."

"Ah, yes, I recognize you from one of your past lives as a villain," smiled the bald Elder whom I had decided to nickname Liberace.

"You robbed my stagecoach at sword point, and weren't above wounding a guard or two to discourage argument." I did not recall the incident, but knew of the lifetime. As a robber, I was proud of my skills with

7

sword and lock pick, though none too proud of the parasitic nature of that chosen profession.

"Bernard, perhaps you would prove useful with the dementia epidemic that rages in the city of Geasa, on the planet Fantibo," the attractive woman stated. Her words struck me as being said for my benefit alone. This must have been the reason behind the Council's call for delegate candidates. Facing an epidemic would be a new challenge. Suddenly, I was hungry with a thousand questions.

"Over a third of the city's population has died, while another third is in the throes of the first stages of the disease," explained the large Elder. "We can project you there; however, your return will be up to you."

This said, he reached across the table and handed me a stack of currency. Then he added, "Bernard, you will receive more than ample support from this Council. However, be mindful—there is a need for haste. Right now, we are in the midst of unusual solar activity. The atmospheric conditions created by these radiations require your projection to Geasa within the hour. You will have only seven days to complete the assignment. If you do not return within the week ..." he paused to consider his words. "... well, the next time you will most likely be able to safely teleport back to this solar system won't be for at least another year."

II

I WAS ELATED. Now was neither the time to puzzle over what I could accomplish in a week, nor how I might occupy myself for a year. I paused and mentally directed the weight of my unanswered questions into an energy of trusting myself, my abilities, Agoragon and the Grand Council. I quickly stashed the cash and quieted my mind with a series of deep, connected breaths. Then I nodded that I was ready. A bright spiral of light exploded behind my eyes, and I was instantly teleported to a lush parkland that overlooked a city.

Skyscrapered Geasa, I presumed, as my head cleared and my surroundings came into sharper focus. There was a subdued buzz coming from the distant city, similar to the sound of a winter-hushed beehive. In the bright sky, a mild breeze rounded up herds of cumulus clouds and ushered them into the distance. Fresh scented, the air was tinged with the sweetness of flowers in their season. To my surprise, standing next to me was the attractive Elder from the Council.

She smiled, said hello and then went back to silently surveying the scene below.

The woman's presence was reassuring. Obviously, the promise of Council support for this mission would be much more that merely financial.

Speaking aloud, the woman introduced herself as Nandia. "I am told that subterranean mineral deposits here in Geasa emit a radiation that is disruptive to telepathic communication. The sound of our voices will help us avoid confusion." After a moment's pause to let that sink in, she asked, "Do you mind if I call you Bernard?" Her voice was soft, melodic and alluring.

"My friends call me Bearns," I replied. "I much prefer it to the longer version." Upon hearing my familiar name, Nandia quizzically raised an eyebrow. It happens. More often than I'd care to admit. But, right now, before me, stood a woman who was quite a woman to behold. Her unusual eyes again caught my attention. They brought to mind my favorite gemstone, a blend of azurite and malachite. It is a vibrant, blue-green stone that I sometimes use to magnify the energies of healing and heart-centered emotions.

Rather than let myself get lost in those eyes, I tore my gaze away, only to find myself falling into the beauty of Nandia's lips. They appeared to have been sculpted as if sensuality were life's only passion. But, my hunger for answers to this mission's thousand questions intruded at just that moment. I quickly muted the flush of delight I felt at being here in Geasa with this Elder.

Instead, I returned to the scene in front of us. "So,

this is the place where insanity is running amok?" I asked.

"I think they would prefer that we call it dementia," Nandia replied dryly. Perhaps she had anticipated my next question, for she went on to explain, "Prior to your arrival at the Council chambers, the Elder you've dubbed as Liberace briefed me on Geasa's problems." I had been wondering how she'd learned of the city and its epidemic.

"This is home to over a million souls," she continued, as she looked out over the city. "They are descendents of a human migration that happened eons ago. Throughout their past, Geasans have refused to accept the idea of multiple lifetimes. So, most live their days shrouded in the fear of death. Naturally, this leaves them feeling isolated and weak. As a panacea, they follow the very conservative Omniversia religion, which, in turn, leaves them terrified of a vengeful, punishing God."

I suspected that such a combination would not bode well for a quick, easy resolution to the problem of an epidemic.

But that realization paled quickly, as this woman's gently lilting voice echoed in my mind. Her tone kindled a desire to grow closer. I watched for a sign that she could sense how I felt. But seeing no reaction, I began to relax. Perhaps Geasa's mineral deposits really did disrupt telepathy. Or, maybe, Nandia was simply ignoring what was going on inside of me.

"Most Geasans don't believe in telepathy," she evenly stated. "Probing their minds, usually what you will find is the attitude, 'My thoughts and feelings aren't important. They don't matter. I'm better off hiding them from you.'"

Hearing that only renewed my doubts. Was I really hiding my attraction for this woman?

"So, is there a medical name for this epidemic?" I asked, not wanting to create any further distractions from the problem at hand.

"It's a viral disease called Saragalla. It was named after a region to the north of Geasa, believed to be where the virus originated. The bad news is, medical experts blame children as being the initial carriers of the disease. Their theory is that truant children, after wandering through the marshlands of the Saragalla Valley, returned to their classrooms carrying the virus. Since then, the disease has grown to epidemic proportions while public outrage at children has spread like wildfire. Many have been banished from their homes. There are even reports of youngsters being shot at when approaching Geasa's outlying farms."

This sobering revelation triggered an urgency in me to find out how we could help. "So, what are the symptoms of Saragalla?" I asked.

"The disease starts with a sudden onset of anemia, deep fatigue, mental exhaustion, drooling and deteriorating speech. These symptoms get progressively worse until severe dementia sets in. Victims fall into deep depression after four to six weeks and resort to violent and self-harming behaviors. Many commit suicide. The Saragalla epidemic is destroying the economic and social fabric of Geasa. The good news is, there have been only a few cases reported elsewhere on the planet."

With the help of several deep, connected breaths, I decided to set aside my heartache over Geasa's scapegoated children. Instead, I recalled what I knew of the Borna disease, a similar viral infection we had back on Earth, my home planet. It was only after the disease had become an epidemic that researchers discovered that the Borna virus had combined with an inherited weakness caused by the syphilis bacteria. The predominant symptom of this genetic weakness was identified as the Dr. Jekyll/Mr. Hyde-type of personality. People so affected were at one moment affable and cooperative, while at the next, angry and hostile. Over time, the condition was so common that it came to be considered the social norm. It was discovered that a number of additional emotional disturbances resulted from this combination of the Borna virus and the genetic taint of syphilis. The epidemic lasted well over six decades.

Thirty years or so after the epidemic began, a small group of healers with whom I was associated came up with an electromagnetic frequency for the disease. Using a radionics instrument, we imbued that frequency into water to create an electromagnetic remedy. This we distributed to people afflicted with the Borna/syphilis combination. It proved to be amazingly effective. Many people taking the remedy had quick success at healing emotional imbalances.

As I recalled the faces of those people, my earlier feelings of frustration returned. We needed to quickly resolve the telepathic disruptions that were being caused by Geasa's mineral deposits. Were it not for that problem, Nandia would now know about Saragalla's similarities to the Borna disease.

"I wonder if there's a way to neutralize this damnable obstacle to telepathy?" I asked.

"I'm not sure; let's experiment," came Nandia's reply. She pulled a crystal pendulum from within the folds of her gown and started with the obvious question.

"Is there an antidote for this interruption to telepathic communications?" she asked. Immediately, the pendulum began swinging clockwise.

"Oh, damn," Nandia cursed. "Clockwise for me means neither yes nor no. It's my pendulum's indication that there's some impedance between my subconscious and conscious minds. Whatever is interrupting telepathic messages is very likely blocking our dowsing, too."

I was trained in the ancient art of dowsing myself. "Daily practice, Bernard, daily practice," Agoragon had repeatedly urged. "It's a powerful discipline to train your conscious mind to access the unlimited information within your Inner Self."

I pulled out my brass pendulum and repeated Nandia's question. My device swung to a dead stop, its indication of the same dowsing impedance she had identified. Then, I remembered a discovery made decades earlier by an aged water diviner, and related the story to Nandia.

"The old dowser told me how he once had been so proud of his impeccable record. Throughout decades of water divining, he had never failed to locate underground water. But, then came the day when he dowsed not one, but three successive dry wells.

"The drilling crew grew so disgusted, they finally

threw in the towel and packed up their rig. Chagrined, the dowser refused to accept his normal fee from the landowner, but did ask for a few dollars to cover travel expenses. Handing over the cash, the owner expressed a regret that he hadn't gone into mining. He knew there was a valuable zinc deposit located just a few feet beneath the surface of his farm.

"That tidbit of information stuck in the dowser's mind. He went back to his lab and began experimenting with zinc. He discovered that the mineral somehow hindered dowsing. But then he discovered the remedy as well: When he wore copper on the left side of his body, it neutralized zinc's disruptive effects.

"So much for the elderly diviner's tale," I concluded. "It makes me wonder if that's what is going on here?"

Smiling, Nandia replied, "Makes sense, Bearns. It occurs to me that zinc could also be aggravating the Saragalla epidemic. Large doses are toxic to the body and disrupt its metabolization of copper, which is consistent with certain Saragalla symptoms. Let's see about finding some copper."

We studied Geasa's skyline as we set out for the city, eager to find a shop that sold trinkets or jewelry made of the metal. Initially, we tried to teleport, but that proved to be fruitless, as well. "It seems that teleportation is being thwarted by the same concentrations of zinc that are interrupting dowsing and telepathy," I speculated.

"Sounds right," Nandia said. "Let's go with that theory, at least until we find out if copper will restore our dowsing abilities. Then, hopefully, we'll learn more."

Unable to use my pendulum, I felt like a frustrated fish trying to swim through mud. Again, I reminded myself to breathe deeply.

Nandia pointed out a tall, gold-domed building off in the distance. We decided to use it as a lodestone to guide our steps, hoping for a harvest of trendy, spendy jewelry shops.

Suddenly, shouting arose from far across the park. A bunch of maybe a dozen youths were running across the green, barking curses and brandishing cudgels. Strollers in the area scurried for the safety of nearby streets. The gang appeared to be made up of street urchins. They looked underfed, unkempt and feral. Ignoring everyone near their path, they loped, pack-like, across the lawn toward their unseen destination.

"Isn't it amazing that these rascals seem immune from any worry of being challenged?" I asked. "Could the fabric of Geasa be unraveling so fast that this pack of predators is free to roam like wolves?"

Nandia considered the question. "It is not unheard of," she answered. "During epidemics, children of families that have been ravaged by disease often band together for survival. It could well be a sign that the city is tottering toward anarchy. Let's hurry, and on our way, take care to watch our backs."

It appeared the city's social structures were deteriorating faster than anticipated. I was anxious to discover how deeply the disease was imbedded within Geasa's culture, and decided to dowse the question. As I reached for my pendulum. I cursed aloud. How silly of me to forget, even for a moment, that my dowsing ability currently lay buried somewhere beneath Geasa's mineral deposits. Nandia took a deep breath as she heard me swear. That was enough to remind me to do the same. The blessed relief of deep breathing!

"My mentor, Agoragon, spent our first year together teaching me how to breathe," I said as we hurried toward the city. "I grew weary of him extolling the virtues of oxygen's cleansing power. He would playfully smile whenever I became mired in self-doubt, usually worrying over failure or lack of approval. Without a word, he would begin deep breathing, continually connecting full inhalations with complete exhalations. Some days, it took hours before I caught on. Finally I came to trust how fundamental the discipline of deep breathing is to healing."

"After a time, I could automatically respond to stress with deep, connected breaths. Agoragon then began teaching me about the ancient Essenes. These were people renowned for their spiritual awareness, healing abilities and capacity to see into the future. Their scrolls revealed that they knew much about the powers of nature and the power of the breath. They honored the air's ability to carry wisdom, instantly and with great compassion, anywhere throughout the world. They tapped into the fundamental power of acceptance by connecting with the consciousness of water. They taught how to heal unhappiness by communing with the energy of life. They were a people of peace—peace with their bodies, peace with nature, with all of humankind, as well as the domains of spirit.

"As I integrated these ideas more deeply into my life, I discovered that nature's elements are not only powerful, but alive and conscious. To this day, I frequently ask these powers for insights into unsolved problems and unfulfilled desires. I am forever grateful

17

to Agoragon for how deeply the Essene wisdom has nurtured my growth."

"He sounds like a remarkable teacher," Nandia replied. "Was it he who taught you dowsing?"

"No, when I was eight years old, a water diviner taught me to locate water by using L-shaped divining rods. Later, Agoragon encouraged me to master the pendulum. He said that by combining my dowsing with breathing exercises, my conscious mind would more easily cooperate with the intuitions of the Inner Self."

Nandia talked of similar teachings. "Like Agoragon, my teacher taught that dowsing is an excellent way to meld our two types of awareness. She often reminded me to release the authoritarian hold I had bestowed upon my intellectual mind. Many long days were spent rooting out limitations I'd planted in my consciousness that were blocking the flow of intuition emanating from my Inner Self. She encouraged practices that married the intellect with the intuitive mind. She said that both types of awareness would grow beyond imagination if only we would build a strong, cooperative relationship between them."

That was exactly what Agoragon had been hoping I'd learn.

We slowed as we reached the hub of the city, navigating through rivers of traffic and waves of people. Geasa was quieter than cities back home, in large part because they didn't have our noisy, infernal combustion machines. Tall buildings were adorned with vertical gardens complemented by curves of glass and chrome—designs that softened the otherwise harshly towering skyscrapers. Signage and traffic signals were

written in Versalia, the language most understood throughout this galactic sector. And, there was a scent of dust in the still air that was tainted with the feeling of gloom.

But it was mostly the crowds that caught our attention. People were subdued, silently moving from here to there. Shoppers at outdoor market stalls listlessly picked through wilted produce and days-old flowers. With hunched shoulders, they seemed to be saying, "Do not intrude. I seek solace in isolation." Their desperation was palpable, as if uncertain how to survive the gathering storm they knew to be looming beyond the horizon. I glanced at Nandia. Her face mirrored my concerns.

Turning to our task at hand, we searched shop windows, looking for copper. After dismissing several shops, we found ourselves standing at the entry of a large, upscale jeweler. "The Opulatum," declared its glittering, cursive sign.

We stared through its double-wide glass doors at the ridiculously gilded shop. It was ablaze with countless prismatic reflections that emanated from crystals dangling from a huge chandelier. We stepped inside and began shopping the glass counters, looking for anything made of copper. Glancing at Nandia, I could see her brow furrow with growing doubt. Passing the last of the elegant displays, we realized that none of the expensive-looking baubles were made of the metal we sought.

A handsome, dapper gentleman approached and said, "Ah, visitors from another planet, I see. I welcome you. My name is Pimpant, Hugh Pimpant. I have the pleasure of being the owner of The Opulatum. We are the most exclusive supplier of precious gems and rare metals in all of Geasa. How may I be of service?"

In an engaging voice, Nandia answered, "We seek a medallion or bracelet made of copper. Although we see none in your displays, I'm wondering if you have any for sale?"

Shock sharpened Pimpant's chiseled face. Putting a finger to his lips, he whispered, "It is illegal for individuals to own copper here."

He gestured for us to follow him and led us to a back office. There, we were well out of earshot from the clerks and customers who had begun examining us with a newfound interest. After shutting the door, he turned to explain. "Our police are quite eager to arrest any merchant who sells copper.

"Three years ago, the government began confiscating the rare metal. For centuries, it has been the real wealth behind our currency. Confiscation began after government debt soared out of control. It has been said that fearful politicians found it easier to simply print more money than to make the difficult decisions necessary to balance their accounts. Meanwhile, a bounty has been offered for any information leading to the recovery of illegal copper. The police doggedly chase all rumors that might lead them to hidden caches of the metal."

Contritely, Nandia adopted an apologetic tone. "Mr. Pimpant, I'm very sorry to have spoken out. We had no idea of copper's value in this society. I hope we have not put you or your establishment at any risk."

"Please allow me to excuse myself and see if there's any need for damage control." He quickly left the room.

I shrugged at Nandia. "Since copper is a proscribed

metal," I suggested, "the only place we'll find any will be on the black market. I wonder if Pimpant could help us."

Nandia nodded. "I'll ask him when he comes back."

Moments later, he returned, looking relieved. "I think I've convinced my employees that you two are on your way to a masquerade ball, and just playing silly pranks on an old family friend." He sounded guarded even as he tried to reassure us. "I've instructed them to gently diffuse any concerns our customers may have."

"I'm sure you were quite convincing," Nandia said. "Please let us know if there is anything we can do to help."

As he thanked her, he relaxed a bit. Nandia then leaned forward and quietly said, "We have no desire to compromise your position any further, Mr. Pimpant. Yet, we are in need of some small copper token. It is necessary in order for us to begin working on the Saragalla plague that has befallen your city. Might you be able to help?"

Pimpant glanced at Nandia with suspicion, as if imagining us to be undercover police. He paused, but then seemed to resolve some inner conflict. The troubled look on his face changed to one of relief. He walked around his desk and sat down, inviting us to take the two chairs opposite him.

"It would be most welcome if you could aid us in our troubles," Pimpant sighed. "The Saragalla epidemic is spreading quickly. The latest research indicates that Geasa will last little more than a year before being completely wiped out. Those still healthy watch with dread as more and more loved ones succumb to this nightmare.

"You both must assure me that you did not hear this from me," he murmured conspiratorially. Leaning toward us, he waited until we had nodded before continuing. "I have a cousin named Raphael, who is a priest at St. Paul's cathedral. Because of the church's occasional need for copper ornaments, he deals with a black marketeer. St. Paul's holds services at three o'clock every afternoon. Sit in the second-last pew on the left side, facing the altar. Do not approach him. Wait there after the service concludes and, in time, he will come to you. Make sure to take plenty of money."

III

AFTER POLITELY THANKING PIMPANT, we said our goodbyes. Outside The Opulatum, we decided to use some of the currency provided by the Council—we needed outfits that would help us blend in. And we were growing hungrier by the minute. We came upon a raw-food restaurant, went in and seated ourselves at their window counter.

Watching the passersby outside, Nandia exclaimed, "Bearns, I've just had one of my feeling-tones about our future! Something's telling me that if we watch the street as we eat, fortune will smile upon us and we'll discover something that will well serve the job at hand." Not only did that leave me curious, but wondering if she had been an Essene in an earlier life.

We ordered full-meal salads, and were pleased to see our plates overflowing with a colorful array of vegetables. I tasted what I thought was an avocado, only to be surprised by the flavor of a carrot. "Most likely a carracado," I chuckled, as I explained its taste to Nandia.

"And this is probably a broccapple," Nandia laughed as she bit into the green floret skewered on her fork. While it looked like broccoli, she swore it tasted like the most familiar fruit.

We talked of Pimpant, of course, and questioned his motives. "It strikes me as odd that his suspicions vanished into thin air only moments after you asked if he could help us find copper," I observed.

"I had exactly the same reaction," Nandia agreed. "And why would he so easily trust us not to reveal his identity after disclosing a source for illegal copper? That, as well, seems quite curious." We decided to approach the meeting with Father Raphael with caution. Then, the conversation turned to the social forces that have stimulated the growth of the Omniversia religion on so many planets.

"I find it extraordinary that the church's teachings have survived," I observed. "As young child, I was quite devoted to the religion. I thought it was the only way to explore the spiritual side of life. At seven years old, I began serving mass as an altar boy. After services one day, a priest walked me the length of the empty church, his arm around my shoulders. I thought he was being friendly until he kissed me. I immediately withdrew and was suspicious toward the clergy ever after. It came as no surprise that the papacy deteriorated years later, after revelations of decades of abuse and financial misconduct."

Nandia moved closer and whispered, "Bearns, I think our energy fields are changing. While you were talking, I noticed that I could telepathically hear your thoughts again. I wonder what is happening?"

As I listened to Nandia, I had to agree that I, too, was hearing her inner expressions more clearly. Her words were shaded with more feeling, an indication of a clearer telepathic connection. It was as if a cloud were lifting from my mind. Dumbfounded, I looked down at my plate. I silently asked my subconscious to help me understand the change. I found myself focusing intently on our salads.

"Of course," I exclaimed aloud, excited with sudden insight. I quickly ducked my head as other diners looked our way. Leaning toward Nandia, I telepathed that kale, cashews and avocados are all high in copper. It could be true for brocapples and carracadoes as well. Whatever the cause, we were getting enough copper to override the prevailing zinc disruptions. We'd discovered one way to revive our telepathic connection!

Silently, we considered this revelation as we savored the salad and listened to each other's thoughts. I could feel my mental energy clarifying and expanding. Pulling out my pendulum, I asked if our search for copper would benefit our investigations into Geasa's epidemic. It swung briefly into the positive position and then returned to neutral. I interpreted this as an indication that the benefits of our food-borne copper would be short-lived. This, I also confirmed using my pendulum.

Nandia nodded and said, "It's quite obvious that we need a real copper item to effectively neutralize zinc."

"Damn, damn and double damn," I cursed. "I had high hopes that a copper-rich diet was all we needed to recover our dowsing abilities. You're right, of course, we must have the metal. The trouble is, we both question the wisdom of expecting a black-marketeering priest, who is also Pimpant's cousin, to help us find illegal copper."

I stared out the window, mentally gnawing at that bone of a worry, when a colorful busker wearing a bright, plaid kilt danced by. Adorned in what could only be described as a coat of many colors, he blazed away on a brass horn, playing a soulful, jazzy tune. A giant of a man, with flaming red hair, he seemed as out-of-place as a showgirl in a convent. Yet, he exuded joy as he jived down the street. People stopped and stared, slack-jawed and wide-eyed. A few even smiled. Mesmerized, I watched the musician until he rounded the corner and disappeared from sight.

I enjoyed my delight at the unexpected musician until my worries over copper crept back into my mind. But, I knew there was no gain in focusing on troubling mental energies when I had no solution. That path only increased the possibility of failure. So, remembering that energy always follows thought, I mentally touched my doubt and asked the energy within it to transform itself into an effective, graceful outcome. I felt a light rush of release as I returned to Nandia and our talk about the Omniversia religion.

"I'm continually amazed that so many societies do not understand that illness is largely dependent upon the distorted beliefs of unworthiness, guilt and punishment," I telepathed. "They have yet to learn that the only way disease can occur is when individual self-respect and self-expression have been compromised. Omniversals must have encouraged such distortions for generations in order for Saragalla to have reached such epidemic proportions."

Nandia agreed. She began projecting mental pictures of her childhood on her home planet of Praesepe. I saw images of classrooms where she was studying mathematics, music, art and ancient languages. A woman in a cleric's robe stood teaching at the head of the class. In one scene, the child Nandia was learning of the history of the church, going back hundreds of years on Praesepe. Those scenes were of people being burned at the stake, children being molested and women persecuted.

Noticing my growing sadness at these horrors, she said, "Our planet outlawed the Omniversals after that era. For many years afterwards, its followers were hunted down and persecuted. Finally, the religion lost its hold. A gentler, nature-based theology grew in its stead, one that taught us of our spiritual connection with nature and respect for its cycles. We learned to respect the unique value of each individual rather than impose the fear of failure, guilt and punishment upon each other."

Tilting my head toward hers, I talked more about the damaging church teachings I had learned. "Omniversia encouraged the notion that people are born bad, unworthy and unlovable. We were taught that individual worth was undermined by failures and mistakes. Clarifying the concept of sin became a big business. The only way to repair such transgressions was to accept guilt, blame and punishment. It's no wonder so many of us are plagued with unhappiness and disease.

"After many years, social behaviors emerged that attempted deal with the diminishment of individuals. One notorious example was a phenomenon called 'political correctness,' a socialized attempt to encourage the expression of respect. Doomed to failure, the new standard was based on the mistaken notion that changing a word symbol would automatically change a speaker's intent. Over time, it became obvious that political correctness was often used to mask expressions of blame, judgment and condemnation. All of which did little to remedy the crisis in self-respect that was undermining people's self worth.

"Similarly, Omniversalist teachings have not been very successful in leading people to greater expressions of their own spiritual nature. Instead, they have fostered the belief that we all are merely powerless victims. Greed, fear, emotional dependencies and self-destructive behaviors have become the social norm."

Nandia nodded and said, "On Praesepe, mistakes and failures are seen as constructive, self-generated opportunities for learning. Our children are being educated to believe that every person chooses this lifetime because of its unique probabilities to grow and contribute. We have no problem assuming that everyone has a passion to uniquely change the world for the better. Individual desires, talents and inclinations are nurtured.

"I see from your childhood memories, Bearns, that you had an early difficulty with math and a passion to draw pictures. I also see that certain nuns encouraged you to mistrust your artistic talent and sought to shame you whenever you failed at math. At home, we would have been horrified to see a child treated so.

"Any child would react the way you did, Bearns— with intense feelings of anger and rebellion. And could it be that you are still blaming those nuns for the guilt you felt about your reactions? I, also, strongly sense a guilt over the doubt and mistrust you imposed upon your own talents."

Feeling a twinge of sorrow over that early childhood conflict, I realized that Nandia's question was a gem. I needed to honestly consider that I was blaming nuns for choices I had made. On a whim, I leaned in and hugged Nandia. As our heads touched, it became clear that talking together was stimulating a deep healing of childhood hurts.

As we parted, I caught sight of the cafe's clock. It was time to get to St. Paul's church. I set aside my desire to learn more of Nandia's life. There was more we needed to learn from the priest Raphael.

We enjoyed our telepathic clarity as we paid the check and stepped out into the street. But, wanting to conserve our newfound energy, we decided to walk rather than teleport to the church. After asking directions, several bystanders pointed out the cathedral steeple that towered over the nearby buildings.

It wasn't long before we were standing in front of the majestic stone edifice of St. Paul's. Pastel-colored spires and flying buttresses complemented its wide, stone-stepped portico. Flanking this entry stood tall, marble statues of Omniversal's saints, arrayed as if blessing all who stepped within its ornately carved doors.

Once inside, we admired the church's elaborate gilt-edged archways and bright, leaded-glass windows that colorfully depicted scenes from church history. The domed nave of St. Paul's would easily accommodate many hundreds of parishioners. Alone, but for the few parishioners whose arrival had preceded ours, we sat as instructed by Pimpant. We watched as one altar boy carefully placed cruets, filled with water and wine, beside the altar. Another lit candles. The incense-laden air was cool and musty.

I felt my mind's vibrant energy slowly ebbing. It was as if it was being shrouded in a dark fog. Obviously, the effects of our copper-rich diet were beginning to fade. Again, I resolved to quickly find the metal we needed, and took comfort in our discovery of foods that could mute, at least temporarily, Geasa's zinc disturbances.

More people arrived, many of whom looked pale and listless. Worry lined their faces. Some knelt and began to pray silently. There was none of the jostling and whispering that often accompanies a congregation's early arrival. It seemed as if some suffocating fear was smothering the life out of these people.

As we waited, we caught glimpses of each other's thoughts. I wondered if the fear we were seeing was in reaction to the epidemic. "I think the source is deeper," Nandia telepathed. "Most likely, originating from the belief that the afflicted are guilty of some transgression and therefore deserve God's wrath."

The church filled with parishioners, and the service began.

An aging, decrepit priest led the submissive congregation through a series of prayers, interspersed with dirge-like hymns. Steadying himself on a wooden handrail, he mounted an elevated pulpit to deliver his sermon. I was shocked to hear that the city's epidemic was divine retribution for its inhabitants' evil lives. People listened with bowed heads. Stunned, I shut out the priest's words by silently repeating the affirmation, "I only respond to constructive suggestions."

Nandia tilted her head in my direction, and I mentally heard the thought, "value fulfillment." Agoragon had used that phrase when he introduced me to the idea that all consciousness ultimately grows in the direction of its greatest fulfillment. Given the strong self-doubt of my childhood, I had initially found it difficult to trust such an idea. So, the timing of Nandia's message was helpful. I shifted my point of view to consider that the Saragalla epidemic was Geasa's best expression of value fulfillment at the present time. As the service ended, I watched people as they filed out of the church. I conceded that I could view their troubles as part of some greater fulfillment they sought as a community. As I changed my thinking, I re-energized my mind.

We waited in the empty church for a quarter of an hour or so, talking quietly about the concept of value fulfillment.

Nandia told of what she had learned. "Remember, even the cells of our bodies are precognitive. They are capable of perceiving the future. And, the Inner Self knows that the future holds infinite probabilities. We create our realities in this world by selecting from this array of probable futures only those outcomes that contribute to our greatest fulfillment. Often this work is done during dreamtime, with the Inner Self and the subconscious working collaboratively.

"Value fulfillment is not only about the fulfillment of each individual consciousness," she concluded. "It's about the fulfillment of all of creation, as well. For some reason, Geasa has selected this probability because it will best serve individual and collective growth."

"That's quite right, young lady." From behind us, a resonant, yet gentle, male voice agreed. "And that, we call God's love."

Startled, we both quickly turned. I wondered how long he'd been there. The tall, middle-aged priest sat down beside us. I immediately noticed a similarity to Pimpant—minus at least a stone's worth of his cousin's girth.

"It's safe to talk here," he assured us after brief introductions. "Cousin Hugh sent a secure message explaining the reason for your visit. I might be of aid in your quest to overcome our scourge of Saragalla. At midnight, I will take you to a seller of copper. Please be aware that you face the risk of being arrested. If you are willing to take that chance, you will need to bring at least ten thousand rhyals. And, I do have a special request in return for this service."

"Father Raphael, what would that be?" I asked and then mentally posed a quick question to Nandia: "Arrested?!!"

"Not your first time, nor mine," her telepathic quip was delivered with a straight face.

Behind a fist and a cough, I suppressed a smile, as I recalled my lifetime as a bandit.

Father Raphael continued, unabated. "I would like each of you to assist me for at least three days at the Saragalla hospice we have here. We're desperately short-handed, and the experience would prove to be invaluable. Saragalla is still mostly a mystery to us. There's been scant time to research its causes."

Nandia and I glanced at each other for confirmation, and then nodded.

After thanking him, I went on to explain. "Father, we believe we can slow down, and then reverse the onslaught of this disease. We hope to discover and produce effective remedies from local herbal and mineral sources.

"We have been trained to pendulum dowse for these natural remedies and translate their constituents into electromagnetic frequencies." He nodded in understanding and I continued my explanation. "These frequencies we transfer into distilled water with the aid of a radionics instrument. However, we've found that Geasa's zinc deposits are restricting our dowsing ability. This has effectively stalled our attempts to discover Saragalla's causes. Copper, we've discovered, will neutralize this restriction. Once we have created these remedies, we will need help to dispense them to everyone infected with Saragalla."

Breathing deeply, he paused to consider my words. His tone was now softer, yet his words spoken with more focused intent.

"Your arrival is an answer to many people's prayers," his message sounded heartfelt. "The nuns and staff working at the hospice will gladly be available to help administer treatment."

As I listened to his voice, I found myself dismissing my worries about illegally seeking copper and decided to trust him further.

He went on to say, "There's a small apartment located behind the sanctuary; please make it your home while you are here."

I telepathed a mental "Yes." to Nandia, who said, "Your generosity, Father, solves one of our most pressing problems. Could you give us time to do more investigating and we'll return this evening?" We made arrangements to meet later, and, repeating our gratitude, we bade each other farewell.

Nandia and I needed time to talk, to plan and to rest. Both of us yearned for the tranquility and rejuvenation of being in nature. We decided to retrace our steps to Geasa's parkland, with a short detour to the outdoor market we'd passed earlier. There, we collected several bags of cashews, kale and carracadoes. Resuming our hike, Nandia gaily spoke of anticipating the luxury of being cushioned on a bed of thick, green grass. A shady spot beneath a grove of tall trees beckoned. With broad-leafed canopies, their branches sprouted aerial roots similar to Banyan trees from home. We were both ready to be off our feet.

I wanted to talk about making Saragalla remedies, a ten-thousand rhyal meeting with a black marketeer and working at the hospice. But, instead, I rested—stretched out next to the trunk of a tree and took in the sun-kissed, cloud-chased beauty of the blue sky.

Agoragon's face flashed across my mind. He was breathing deeply and alternately closing each nostril. I sent a mental note of thanks and began a series of alternate nostril breaths—a single inhalation through the left nostril, then a complete cycle of exhalation and inhalation through the right. I alternated sides by pinching off the unused nostril. The exercise ran through a count of twelve breaths. Agoragon taught the discipline as an energy-gathering exercise. He told me it was once used on Earth to promote physical immortality.

As I lay supine upon the lush, shaded lawn, I relaxed and continued deep breathing. There were several unfamiliar birdsongs in the distance. Closing my eyes, I allowed myself to melt into that music. I could feel my mental and physical energies being restored, batteries recharged. There was an emerging sensation of fear tugging at my abdomen. I directed my breath to touch that spot. It was a fear of failing at this mission, of losing the opportunity to serve as a Council delegate. It was asking for my attention. In a half-dream state, I heard my mentor's voice, again, remind me that energy always follows thought. With that in mind, I asked the energy within the fabric of the fear to transform itself into trust—trust that all of our actions are guided by the law of value fulfillment.

I opened my eyes, delighted to see a renewed vibrancy in nature's beauty. I wanted to spend all afternoon enjoying this experience, especially the sight of Nandia as she lay sprawled across the grass.

"Hey, Sleepyhead, are you ready to ease the weight of all those unanswered questions?" she smiled as she rolled over and propped herself up on an elbow.

"This moment's peace is quite rare," I said softly. "I hate to abandon it to the matters at hand."

"Oh?" The musical tone in her voice invited me to say more.

"Yes, I ask that every step of this journey be consistent with my ideal of self-respect. I can't see how pursuing copper illegally will fit. Meeting a black marketeer puts us at risk of arrest, which would compromise our relationship with the police. Their help may well be needed if we are to get our as-yet unborn remedies to the thousands of people afflicted with Saragalla. My inclination bone itches, urging me to at least postpone this meeting. Can we trust there's a better way to find the copper we need?"

Lighthearted, Nandia was playful in her response. "Yes, oh Great Galactic Traveler," she continued, her voice lilting. "It is wisdom itself to assure that one's steps dance gracefully along life's path. I see you are learning to trust that growth is the only direction energy flows. I, too, could never use a means to resolve Geasa's epidemic, if such a means meant compromising our ideals."

I had to chuckle, appreciative of Nandia's easy reassurance of value fulfillment. Feigning a serious gaze, I innocently asked, "Any thoughts on how we might otherwise cop some copper?"

In her melodic voice, Nandia answered, "We can trust, Bearns, that our shared ideals are meant to polish and purify the means we select to reach them. So, let's trust we will easily attract that elusive, vagabond copper, and transform the energies within your worry and doubt into the delight of being a topper copper-shopper."

Even though I shuddered at her butchered doggerel, it seemed another bird had sung.

IV

LYING AMID THE PARKLANDS TREES, I struggled with an ache to melt into a romance with Nandia. Then, I remembered that we had yet to find a way to produce our vibrational remedies. We needed to find a radionics instrument. I focused on breathing, let myself relax and imagined an unknown source fulfilling that need, at just the right time.

I felt the warmth of my heart reaching out to Nandia. Even though I wanted this yearning to grow, I couldn't, in good conscience, compromise the priority of our mission. "What do you say to this idea, Nandia?" I asked. "Let's talk to a police officer and hear their suggestions for finding copper. Who knows, they may even know of a radionics practitioner we could meet."

"Bearns, Bearns," Nandia's raised eyebrows issued a challenge. "Why fight it?" I knew she was referring to the emotional struggle roiling inside of me. "For now, let's put the police on hold. Meanwhile, you might want to accept your heart's feelings as also an expression of value fulfillment. That and the guilt you feel about your affections. You recovering Omniversals! You certainly have a gift for creating inner turmoil."

I'd resisted the fact that I could be so easily read. Not only did I feel a bit chagrined that Nandia was aware of my desires for her, but a bit vulnerable, as well. I did, however, appreciate her gentle touch.

"I do want to say more about how I feel," I admitted. "But I also want more time to sort out my feelings. For now, shall we decide if we want to obligate ourselves to Father Raphael by staying at the church?" We both agreed to the idea. We had much to learn about Saragalla, and would have a roof over our heads.

"One bed or two?" Nandia asked playfully.

"Let's ask for two, each big enough for two," I countered.

I did enjoy the fun of being with Nandia, which was suddenly interrupted as I found myself recalling the street minstrel we had seen earlier.

"I've been wondering about the same man," Nandia replied, catching my thoughts. "How do you feel about him?"

"I'm filled with admiration. He strikes me as one of the few courageous people we've seen here. It's quite remarkable the way he exudes happiness in the midst of Geasa's crisis. I want to meet him. I've a sense he holds at least one key to resolving the epidemic."

"Come on, then. Let's get back to the city and follow his music," she suggested. "I've yet to meet a musician who would turn down an invitation to a meal."

Getting up from the green grass, I wondered if all of our chances to rest would be this brief.

V

CHATTERING LIKE JAYBIRDS, we approached the city. Even though we brainstormed every idea we could imagine, we found none to thaw the paralysis that was freezing our access to copper. While glad to be carrying copper-rich foods, we looked forward to the time when the metal would cross our path. One constant fact dogged our every step: We had only seven days to complete this mission. We could not move forward until we had dowsed the causes of Saragalla. Toward that end, our hunger grew.

We talked about how viral infections are physical manifestations of blocked emotional energy. As we'd seen at St. Paul's, most people wore their fears like yokes strapped across their shoulders. With no idea of their power to heal fear, this bone-chilling emotion was certainly a significant factor in Geasa's epidemic. Again, dowsing would confirm the emotional causes of Saragalla. I found myself wishing that Father Raphael had simply given us several pieces of copper.

But then a nagging discomfort I felt about the

priest came to mind. "A similar sense of disquiet came up earlier," I said to Nandia. "It was during our time with Pimpant. Now, I find myself wondering about the message within those feelings. Earlier, I had put it off to being an off-worlder, unfamiliar with Geasans. I do wish I were able to read their energy fields."

I related to Nandia my perennial disappointment over my inability to see auras. For years, Agoragon had put forward many aura-reading exercises. Despite his best efforts, I failed to make any progress. A child-hood fear returned—that I had some permanent flaw, perhaps some unknown learning disability. That had to be the reason I was so irritably donkey-slow and unable to see energy fields. My discouragement only grew as the years passed. Finally, Agoragon stopped prodding, which I interpreted as, yet, another piece of evidence of some inner flaw.

"Notice how you tend to be a bit hard on yourself about your failings, Bearns?" Nandia gently asked. "You have completely missed the fact that your disquiet about Pimpant and the priest is evidence enough that you are aware of their auras. Your self-diminishment could very well be blocking your ability to expand this inner sense. Perhaps, to best learn this lesson, where you are at the moment is exactly where you need to be. Could you accept that your present state of inability is a useful part of the path to mastering your ability to read energy fields?

"And, I will offer this," she quietly continued. "You must learn to relax your sole dependency upon your physical vision. Sometimes, people feel or even hear energy fields, in addition to seeing them. I noticed that both men's auras were shaded with muddy brown and grey colors. Your instincts were accurate. There is something they were afraid to reveal to us."

It was helpful being reminded of the burden of unworthiness that I bestow upon myself, especially when experiencing failure. Nandia's reassurance suddenly reminded me of an aura-reading experiment suggested by Agoragon years earlier. That memory excited me. With sharp mental focus, I asked my subconscious for assistance in dismissing the attitude of failure I'd been carrying. An unseen, yet familiar, shadow suddenly lifted. Relieved, I turned toward Nandia and asked for her help.

"Dear One, there's an exercise my mentor once suggested, but was never tried. Would you mind helping? He told me that the easiest time to see a person's aura is when they are just about to teleport. He also said it's best to work with someone I care deeply about. Would you mind leaving so I can watch for your energy field?"

She enthusiastically agreed. "Once I'm gone, look for me in front of that tall conifer to the east," she said, pointing to her destination. She was quite confident, as if I was about to learn the easiest thing in the world. We opened up the cache of food from our pockets and ate several carracadoes plus a healthy handful of cashews.

I then relaxed, breathing deeply. Nandia stood facing me, radiant and beautiful. A warm wave of affection swept through me. Suddenly, I began to see a few golden darts of light emanating from around her head! Then, the energy centers of her heart and solar plexus began radiating visible energy. Their colors of green and gold intensified, glowing in a variety of pastel hues. A wave of excitement surged through my belly. Nandia remained stationary for a few moments. As I indulged in a greater intensity of affection for her, I discovered my new-found vision beginning to wane. I began a series of deep, connected breaths and calmed down. This refreshed my ability to see her aura's colors.

Nandia then began fading from sight, until her torso and face were all that remained. Finally, all I could see was a corona of color, its hues slowly melting into the air around her. Then, in the very last moment of watching her aura, her lips gently popped and blew a playful kiss. A warm nudge hit my heart.

I was so surprised from the nudge of that kiss that I almost missed Nandia's reappearance in front of the conifer. Fortunately, her kiss had turned me slightly to my right and I caught sight of muted purples, blues and greens as her aura vibrated with greater intensity. Red and gold hues then began to appear. I remembered to breathe deeply as I reveled in my accomplishment.

Then her body materialized. Physical once again, Nandia laughed, spread her arms wide and skipped toward me. I continued seeing the colors of her aura as she drew near! We met somewhere in the middle—a joyful embrace.

I exuberantly thanked her as we held each other. "For the first time in my life," I exclaimed, "I have observed an energy field disappear and then reappear. And, right now, I'm still able to see your aura's colors!"

"That was great fun, Bearns." Nandia laughed, her face shining. "I think you'll find your ability will grow easily now. But don't expect to be seeing auras every minute of the day. Remember, to use this inner sense, you'll need to set aside judgments and worries to allow the state of inner peace that is needed."

Then a shadow moved across her face. "I don't know why, but I'm now feeling the press of time," she said, frowning. "Let's go find our minstrel and see how he fits into the scheme of things. I agree that later we may need to work with the police department. Yet, in this moment, I've a feeling-sense that befriending this busker will somehow open the door we need to locate copper."

My newfound skill helped us find the musician quickly. Nandia suggested that I relax, visualize his aura and then allow my body to be drawn toward him. When I closed my eyes, it was quite easy to imagine the troubadour's energy field. I saw a large, oval corona reflecting the hues of his many-colored coat. It was crowned in a halo of red, similar to the color of his hair. I then asked my subconscious to assist me in finding its present location. The musician's aura contracted to a point in the sky, beyond the parkland and well into the city. We set off, letting my physical impulses guide us. This was one time I was pleased that we weren't teleporting—our pace of walking helped me explore my intuition's probing for the musician's aura.

As we walked, my mental imaging improved. It became easier to recognize the busker's energy field. Even with my eyes open, it now appeared brighter, multihued and more vibrant with color. His flaming red hair seemed to cast its intensity beyond the halo, into the corona surrounding him. After that, it became a breeze to pick him out from among others in the distance. At times, I had to remind myself to rein in my exuberance, yet, like a dam breaking, it spilled over every time I shared with Nandia the details of what I could see. In those moments, I became a child again.

Like a blind man who recovers his sight, I was impatient to see more. I yearned to examine other people's auras and find out what more I could learn. I especially wanted to watch the energies of Pimpant and Father Raphael, but knew that would have to wait.

After some twisting and turning through city blocks, our search was rewarded. We could hear the busker's music as we came upon a piazza built around a tall bronze sculpture, a rendering of a military officer from Geasa's past sitting astride a prancing horse on parade.

The minstrel was playing his horn at the statue's base. A crowd surrounded him, captivated by his music. In addition to his bright, multi-colored tunic, a hand-stitched jester's cap sat atop his mane of red hair. The colors he wore did correspond to those of his aura. His body was in fluid motion as he played, a study in dance, mesmerizing to watch. While a few bystanders were emulating his moves, others half-heartedly clapped their hands or tapped their feet. These people looked tired and ill. Yet, even they were smiling, their faces brighter than most we had seen this day.

"C'mon, Bearns, let's go sing," Nandia grabbed my arm, pulling me toward the busker.

I planted my feet in protest. I had a rule against singing in front of an audience.

"Trust me, you wabbo-headed ding-dong." Laughing, she tugged harder. This time, I acquiesced. She guided me to a spot to the left of the musician, who nodded at our arrival. Nandia stepped to his right. Then her voice rang out, creating a series of tones that harmonized beautifully with his tune. Despite feeling self-conscious at being stared at by the crowd,

I tentatively added my voice, an octave lower than Nandia's. I breathed in relaxation, let go and let my body produce the sound it wanted. I then picked up the tempo set by the busker. Soon, we were producing a pleasing musical round, my voice lending the deeper notes. I imagined myself as a double bass and began jazzing up my rhythm a bit. Nandia smiled in my direction, the troubadour winked and I realized that this could get to be fun.

We fell into a groove. Faces in the crowd opened up as we improvised. People began moving with a greater vitality. More clapped in time with our music, more began dancing. Some even added their voices to our own. I watched as their auras grew more vibrant and could easily see that their vitality was improving.

Telepathically, I suggested to Nandia that we experiment with musical toning on those afflicted with Saragalla. She nodded in agreement.

After a final jazzy rendition of the song's chorus, the busker closed with an eight-bar reprise of its melody. As that faded into silence, he held up his hand, inviting Nandia and me to follow suit. We waved throughout the crowd's enthusiastic applause. After a final bow, he apologized that he needed to bring our performance to a close. He thanked the crowd for the cash that had made its way into his horn's case, and promised an encore performance very soon.

After the crowd slowly dispersed, we introduced ourselves. I then eagerly talked of the unexpected joy I felt during this, my first public singing performance.

"Aye, Laddie," he said in a rough brogue. "And nary a soul among us had any idea 'twas yer debut." We laughed together at that.

Nandia invited him to share a meal with us. He readily agreed—provided he got to pick the place to eat. Happy to oblige, we fell in step beside him. He guided us in a new direction, toward an unfamiliar part of the city.

He told us his name was Dunstan. Listening to his dialect, I recognized him as a Scotsman, from an ancient and remote civilization back home. In addition to what I'd already observed in his aura, there was a quality to his voice that made it easy to trust him. Nandia spoke of our plan to create a remedy to help heal Geasa's epidemic. She explained that the absence of copper was thwarting our dowsing abilities. Dunstan nodded, listening with great interest.

"We've met Father Raphael of St. Paul's, who has invited us to meet later tonight with a black marketeer who sells the metal," she concluded.

"Hmmm." The tone of dismissal was obvious in Dunstan's voice. "That's a right worry, so it 'tis, but I'm glad you've answered my call." I was momentarily caught off guard as I realized that I had, indeed, heard his message telepathically.

"You're the first person we've found here who is aware of telepathy," I thought, focusing my consciousness his direction. "How could that be?"

He told of having teleported here decades past, only to have the zinc deposits interrupt his ability to return home. For years, he had sought the answer. It was only by chance that he had stumbled upon the benefits of copper, much the same way we had. Recently, he had clairvoyantly realized that help was on the way and been awaiting our arrival ever since.

We talked as we navigated city streets, past upscale

neighborhoods and downsizing businesses. Our meandering took us to the edge of a run-down residential neighborhood. There, abandoned dwellings languished amidst others that were in dire need of maintenance. It was clearly a neighborhood suffering the effects of Geasa's troubled times. We stopped at the front door of a dilapidated house, its condition mirroring that of its neighbors. We waited only briefly after Dunstan rapped on the front door. It opened to reveal a petite, raven-haired hostess who ushered us in. Brightly dressed in a high-necked, vibrantly-colored kimono, she welcomed us, as if we had been expected. Dwarfed by the Scotsman, she tugged on his tunic until he bent to be greeted with a warm kiss to his lips.

She then led us to a private dining area, quite simple, yet elegant. After busying herself with our napkins, she presented us with menus. The meals offered looked nutritious, replete with copper-rich foods.

After we ordered, Dunstan continued his story. He had come to the planet wanting to help loosen the church's hold on Geasa. After finding himself marooned, he realized that his music would contribute to healing in the community. There was a sadness in his eyes that I could see reflected in his aura. I wanted to ask if he regretted his long absence from home, but our hostess interrupted with a tap on his shoulder. She whispered urgently in his ear. I picked up a brief sense of alarm from the musician, who thanked her and then turned back to us.

He reached beneath the neckline of his tunic and retrieved a medallion that was suspended from a silver chain. As he lifted it above his head, I could see that it was of unique design. It was two medallions, in fact, made to cover both the energy center on his chest and the corresponding area on his back. Crudely made and adorned with a curious, semicircular pattern, their brightness had been tarnished by the green tint of oxidation.

"T'is copper," Dunstan said, amused at our surprise. "I've not shown this to another soul. Seven years it took to gather and shape. Since the government's meddling, it has become so valuable that many people would readily kill just to say it 'twas theirs. 'Twill feed a neighborhood for an entire year, so 'twould."

"Try it on," he said, passing it to me. I spent a moment appraising the handmade pendant before passing it to Nandia. She slipped it over her head.

"Now, to business." Dunstan was intent on a problem. He reported that, only moments earlier, the kitchen staff had answered a knock at the back door. "Two rogues, dressed in black, askin' if anyone had seen me with two foreigners in tow. They'd be right villains, so they are, up to who knows what brand of skullduggery. We'll be needin' to watch our backs when we leave, depend on it."

He waited until we had both nodded before explaining the rest of what he knew.

"Raphael has been trapped in the grips of an extortion plot," Dunstan said. "They've forced him to become an informant for a police operation huntin' copper dealers. You'll not be wantin' to be a part of any knittin'-bee between the priest and black marketers, not if you're not wantin' to cruel your pitch and go on the corn, eatin' hominy and porridge in the slammer. Yet, a few coppers are right sympathetic to our cause.

Ya must remember, though, take great care before trustin' any other soul."

"There's a bobby I know who can talk the hind leg off a jackass. He just might help us spread your remedy for Saragalla," he continued. "Aye, there are powerful forces in Geasa who would rather this sickness lay waste this fine city. Thugs have been about their nastiness with me twice already, and I don't reckon 'tis because they're hopin' for more of me lovely tunes. I've been hidin' my telepathic and teleporting skills, and you'd be well advised to do the same. Let's figure that Raphael has already dobbed you into the constables. You'll nae be wantin' them ta be pattin' ya down, not with that medallion 'round your neck."

"But, why do people want to discourage the healing of Saragalla?" I asked.

Dunstan paused, considering the question. "For some time now, powerful ne'er-do-wells within the church and government have been plunderin' Geasa's wealth. They're no saints, I'm sorry to say. Right scoundrels they are; extortin' businesses, layin' on a new crop of outlandish taxes, chargin' rhyals for the sacraments, and confiscatin' assets just for the pure meanness of it. This latest law against owning copper is but part of the blodgers' plan to line their own pockets, the greedy bastards. You're needin' to know that the danger you're in has grown like topsy since ya've been seen in my esteemed company."

Quietly thoughtful during this exchange, obviously Nandia had something on her mind. "These people want a third of the population to die?" she asked, dumbfounded. "How could such tragedy serve their ends?"

"Aye, Lassie, 'tis quite simple, really. With the onset of the Saragalla epidemic, the government not only began confiscating copper. They raised estate taxes seventy-five percent. 'Tis a fantastical avariciousness drivin' these crooks. You can bet your last rhyal that before this epidemic runs its course, we'll see a large-scale exodus of the knaves and their families. They'll be leavin' behind a virtual ghost town, stripped of its life and wealth. That is, unless we can get on top of this disease and put an end to their legalized looting."

Dunstan's aura was broadcasting the strong blue colors of rebellious determination tinged with the muddy browns of hopelessness. I now had a deeper understanding of the despair that was so palpable within the community. I was beginning to feel some of that darkness myself.

"I must remember that I alone am creating my feelings of despair," I said, feeling unsure of myself as I spoke. "It's frightening how easily I can let myself fall into the wasteland of hopelessness. I am reminding myself that my feelings are the physical children of my own thoughts. It helps me more easily throw off the burden of despair."

I worked to bolster my own confidence. "It's impossible to create a feeling of despair that is bigger than I am," I affirmed. Both Dunstan and Nandia nodded in agreement. I could see that they, too, were struggling with the same feelings.

"Even though I see so many goin' off their bloody heads, I trust that the good people of Geasa have created these troubles for some useful purpose," Dunstan added thoughtfully. "It won't do for us to forget that any imbalance we create, we can heal. And, that every healing involves an emotional healing. This healing, like every healing, will challenge us to forego some limitation in our thinking." I thanked him, quite comforted to know we had an ally of such wisdom.

The fiery Scotsman was ready to go. "Seems to me we need to get you two to Raphael's shelter so you can learn more about this epidemic," he said. "Mind you, ya' could be roundin' a turn into a rough trot."

"Thank God for your medallions," Nandia said to Dunstan. "If trouble arises, I could always spirit myself to the statue where we met and we could plan our next moves from there. That is, Bearns, if you're willing to be our sacrificial lamb and molder in a jail cell until we can spring you?"

After a moment's careful reflection, I nodded in assent. I realized that I could trust the pair of them to untangle any trouble that might befall us.

"You'll be creatin' a new problem for yourselves, so you will," Dunstan advised. "Once you inform Raphael that you na' wishin' to meet the black marketeers, he'll surmise you've found some other source for copper. I've long believed that the rascals suspect I'm carryin' some. That would explain their attacks on me. Those medallions have aided my scarpers, but, the bad news is, they have also advertised my abilities. The good news is, the copper has helped me predict the ruffians' evil plans before they can find me. Then it's easy slather to stowaway in one of the many hidey-holes I've found. I'll be showin' ya several on our way to St. Paul's."

Night had fallen by the time we left the restaurant. The air was heavy and chilled. A light rain had begun to fall. Nandia shivered. Noticing her discomfort,

Dunstan draped his colorful jacket across her shoulders. Clasping the garment closer, she smiled in gratitude. I just shivered and began breathing deeply, asking that my subconscious warm my body. It took several minutes, but it worked. I've used the technique often enough, and knew I could rely on it. Like lost children, we clung together as we wove our way through streets and lanes.

The rain grew heavier, the night darker and more foreboding. We were trudging through a dark alley when we came upon the first of Dunstan's hideouts. It was a broken-down wooden shed with a portion of its roof missing. He silently pointed it out, tilted his head toward us and quietly said, "You'll need to make sure you're carrying a torch. This place will keep you well-hidden from any meanness."

I looked down the alley toward a lighted street, where an all-night pub stood opposite the lane's entrance. I marked it as a useful landmark as we continued on.

It was a foul night to be scurrying through the dark. And, even though we'd planned for it, when trouble came, it caught us unawares. Suddenly, with great speed and agility, three men, flashing knives, leapt upon us from behind. Dunstan dove into them, swung his horn in its case and bellowed what sounded like an ancient Gaelic war cry. One of the assailants took the blow to his head and folded like a broken accordion. The others were immediately cautious.

Nandia and I leapt to cover both sides of the giant musician, arms up and ready to deflect deadly blades. To quickly increase power of my blows, I inhaled deeply through my nose and then sharply exhaled through my mouth. As the thugs moved in, I jumped the larger of them, immobilized his knife arm and sent his weapon tumbling into the night. Between them, Nandia and Dunstan trapped the last attacker. I cocked my elbow to deliver a blow to my opponent's throat, when suddenly a searing pain cut through my chest, just below my collarbone. I screamed in frustration as I went down, angry at myself for not checking both of my attacker's hands for weapons. I'd been shot and hadn't heard a sound. I fought to keep from losing consciousness. My assailant turned and ran.

Dunstan disarmed their man. Nandia stepped in and skillfully jabbed two pressure points at the base of his skull. Instantly, he was out for the count.

An intense pain began to throb in my chest. Looking up into the night sky, I saw clouds opening to reveal the stars of an unfamiliar constellation. As I slipped into darkness, the last sounds of the scuffle faded into silence.

VI

I AWOKE TO FIND MYSELF IN A CROWDED and brightly lit medical ward overflowing with beds of people. Crammed around the outside aisles and down the middle of the large room were more beds. Harried medical staff ministered to the bedridden. The walls, ceiling and even the blankets were white. This gave the room an antiseptic, eerie feeling.

My head was throbbing and the wound in my chest ached. I couldn't decide which bothered me the most. From the numbness elsewhere in my body, I knew I'd been given pain killers. Through blurred vision, I could see Father Raphael in the distance, while next to me sat Nandia. The worry lining her face transformed into a smile as she noticed me regaining consciousness.

"How bad is it?" I rasped.

"The bullet passed through, just missing your lung and arteries. There's lots of tissue damage. Dunstan carried you here and Father Raphael had his most skilled team of doctors tending your wounds. Dunstan has gone off to talk with his friend in the police force.

He took along his medallion. He's worried that this latest attack is a sign that the opposition is getting more dangerous and determined."

Dunstan's excursion made sense. As my wound throbbed, my hope intensified that he find more support for our cause. I briefly wondered what had become of our other two attackers, but decided to wait until Nandia and I could have a private conversation. My greatest concern was to heal quickly—I needed to get back on my feet. Rationally, my mind wanted to explore the damage to my body. Yet, from long experience, I knew that attempting to further understand my trauma could easily lead me to visualizing the problem only getting worse.

If there's anything I've learned about healing, it's that a body heals much quicker when it's relaxed than when under stress. I started breathing deeply, calmed my mind and let my voice find the musical tone that resonated with the ache in my chest.

I tried different notes until I felt the one that offered the greatest easing of the pain. Next, I experimented with its volume. I began softly and modulated its strength until I felt further relief from my discomfort. I had just begun humming my note in long, sustained tones when I heard a giggle coming from the bed next to mine. There lay a pretty, raven-haired girl, probably ten years old, dark eyes large and bright in an otherwise pale and drawn face. She was trying to match my tone and laughing at her own clumsiness as her high, soprano voice struggled to sustain a note. Her vocal chords were obviously impaired, one of the symptoms common to Saragalla.

I stopped toning. "Hello," I said. "My name is Bearns, and this is Nandia. Who are you?"

"Ss ..., Ssa ..., Sarah," she stuttered. "Wh ..., Why are you here?" Her speech triggered a painful concern that the progression of the disease could further deteriorate such a young and innocent beauty.

"I got shot by a guy having a bad day," I replied. "Would you like to help me heal my wound?"

She giggled again and nodded enthusiastically. I imagined her time in the hospice bed to be about as appealing as crossing stormy seas in a crowded lifeboat. I was drawn to her laughter and had to admire her strength of spirit.

"With my voice, I'm finding the musical note that will vibrate healing to my wound. So, let's sing together for a bit, and each find a note that feels best to the hurt. OK?" Again she nodded, smiling happily.

I sang the tones of the musical scale, spending a moment on each one until she had found that same note in her range. Nandia joined in, singing in Sarah's octave and gently guiding her to experiment with different sounds. As they each moved through the scale, I smiled and nodded whenever they landed on tones that eased my pain. Soon the three of us had hit a harmony that included the note I had found earlier.

We held our notes together until we needed to breathe, and before long, we were toning like a long-practiced trio. Nandia placed one hand over the bullet's entry point, and the other over the exit wound. It was painful to the touch, yet the discomfort faded quickly as healing energy radiated from her hands.

I closed my eyes and imagined the pain as a group of cells, all of an angry, red color. As I sang, I imagined the red of individual cells transforming into an emerald green. I knew that color visualization accelerate the regeneration of damaged tissues.

The three of us worked together for maybe ten minutes, when Nandia said softly, "I think you're done, Bearns. Would you like to try standing up?"

I opened my eyes, grateful for the release of pain and the renewal of vitality I now felt. I began a series of deep breaths, cautiously swung my legs over the side of the bed and stood up. It worked! I experienced only slight dizziness as I raised up on my toes, and then bent into a deep squat. I continued deep breathing and took a few steps. A sense of physical strength flowed through my body. There was absolutely no feeling of injury anywhere. I danced a few steps in short celebration. Then I hugged Nandia, delighted to have healed so quickly.

I turned to Sarah and thanked her for her help. "Would you like to do more musical toning?" I asked.

"Oh, yes," her face was radiant with joy. "Show me, please."

Nandia took over and helped Sarah find the note that would relieve the catch in her vocal chords. She also placed her hands gently around Sarah's throat, treating the area with healing energy. Within minutes, we could all hear the catch in her voice easing. Her sweet soprano voice became stronger and rang out like a crystal bell. Noticing the improvement, she rewarded us with a very sweet, heartfelt smile. She nodded at Nandia and said, "Thank you. I see how to sing it now."

"Sarah," asked Nandia, "how about if you and I visit others here in the hospice? Together, we could help them learn how to heal with their voices."

But before the youngster could answer, we were interrupted by a doctor who was concerned about the disruption we had created. With a stern look of irritation, he ordered me back to bed. "Sir, please do not leave your bed. A wound such as yours needs at least twenty-four hours of complete bed rest. You've not been here so much as an hour."

"Would you please examine my wound, doctor?" I asked, wanting to sound as innocent as possible. I sat down on the edge of the bed and pointed to the bandage on my chest. He slowly unwrapped the dressing. As the last of blood-stained gauze pads were removed, his eyes flashed wide with surprise. A pink scar was all that remained of the bullet wound.

"That's impossible," he exclaimed, looking confused. "It normally takes at least two weeks for such healing to occur. How did it happen?"

"Well doc, I am a believer that anyone can heal any injury quickly, once they put their minds to it. My teacher once told me that healing doesn't take time, it creates time. Nandia also added some energy healing while the three of us sang to the wound. Would you like to accompany us as we help others learn how to use vocal toning to speed their healing?"

"Oh, yes, Dr. Rosenbloom, please do come with us," Sarah encouraged. "See how much better my voice is since we sang it into health?" A study in eagerness, her face was glowing.

Looking incredulous, the young doctor shook his head. He followed us to the group of children in nearby beds. As Nandia passed by, she quietly said, "Isn't it a joy to see how quickly Sarah has embraced healing? She'll have this entire hospice accepting their healing power in no time." We shared a warm chuckle over that idea.

I tagged along and listened to Nandia as she spoke to each child. After she explained toning, she asked for them to point to the spot in their body where they felt sick. Mostly, it was heads and throats, although several pointed to their mid-backs. Every one of them joined in the fun of toning—clear evidence that singing together, in and of itself, nurtures healing. It restores a sense of belonging and well-being.

Once a child found their musical note, Nandia placed her hands over the area of their discomfort. I added color visualizations as I toned. Each child was asked to tell us as soon as they began to feel better. Some healings took mere minutes, others took a bit longer. Regardless of the time expended, the group of clamoring children grew as Sarah invited each of them to tone with us.

It was a joyful, playful crowd that grew larger as beds emptied. It wasn't long before the rest of the ward was demanding to know what was happening. Despite his earlier skepticism, Dr. Rosenbloom was now beaming like a happy child himself. He stepped ahead of the group and began explaining what was going on to people we'd not yet met.

I became curious and asked the doctor if there were any patients displaying Saragalla's advanced symptoms of rage and self-destruction. He pointed toward a door that was flanked by two guards at the far end of the ward. I quietly asked Nandia if she was happy to accompany the children while I investigated further. "No problem," she laughed. "I wouldn't miss this for the world."

As we approached the guarded room, its two sentries looked up at me with suspicion. Neither of them made the slightest move to allow us entry. Dr. Rosenbloom introduced me as the gunshot victim who had just made a miraculous recovery. The larger of the duo granted me a reluctant nod as he stepped aside and unlocked the door.

I was instantly stunned by the cacophony of noise that assaulted us. The room was full of bedridden patients, ranting and fighting to free themselves from their restraints. More sentries were stationed around outside walls. It was a scene that brought to mind a place back home called Bedlam. Bedlam was a sixteenth-century London neighborhood where tourists paid to watch the ravings of dying syphilitic patients. Some had been treated with mercury, which exacerbated the problem of a deteriorating nervous system. I reminded myself to breathe deeply.

I stopped at the bed of a young man who was raving. He was bathed in sweat, his lips thinly stretched across his teeth while his hands futilely clawed at his chest.

From behind, I heard Dr. Rosenbloom's worried voice. "We're running out of medications to keep these people sedated. Their self-destructive, suicidal ravings go on like this for about a week before their hearts fail. They usually die of cardiac arrest."

I sat next to the young man and slowly began talking in a deep, melodious voice. I told him who I was and that I wished to help him recover his ability to heal. I repeated my words, taking deep breaths as I talked. Then I began singing to him, a favorite Russian lullaby from days long gone by:

> If the people lived their lives,
> as if it were a song for singing out of light,
> provides the music for the stars
> to be dancing circles in the night.

As I continued singing these words, I gently placed my palms over his solar plexus, giving him healing energy. Gradually, his body began to relax. His struggle against his restraints eased. Soon, he fell into a troubled sleep. I sat next to him until the pulsing of energy in my hands began to wane.

Incredulous, Dr. Rosenbloom shook his head and said, "Bearns, if we had a thousand people with your skills, we could beat this thing. But right now, we're having to turn Saragalla victims away, and it's like this in every hospital and hospice throughout the city."

"Will you allow Sarah to help other children teach patients toning and breathing exercises?" I asked.

I knew this was a good way to build momentum for healing Saragalla. The news that disease was not incurable would spread like the wind, building a fountain of optimism within the community. That alone would help speed up Geasa's healing.

"Absolutely," the doctor nodded. There was no trace of doubt in his energy field.

"Terrific." I replied. "Nandia and I are working to find the causes of this disease. It seems to be a combination of several, some embedded within the psyches of its victims. We want to do some dowsing tests with our pendulums to discover vibrational remedies that can reach these causes. We believe such an approach will open inner doors within each of the afflicted, so they can heal themselves. Once that's accomplished, can we count on you and your hospice staff to help us reach out to the rest of the city?"

"I'll get to work," said Dr. Rosenbloom. "Let me see what I can do. The unconventional methods I've seen tonight are proving to be quite effective. What sort of remedy are you considering?"

"Nandia and I want to discover if Geasa's abundant zinc deposits are somehow throwing people's copper metabolization out of balance. It's obvious to us that suppressed emotions and the Saragalla virus itself are among the other causes for the disease. We need more time for our research. Once Saragalla's causes are clear, we can identify their electromagnetic frequencies. After that, it's quite easy to produce safe, effective vibrational remedies using a radionics instrument. However, right now, our greatest need is sleep."

He nodded and led me back to where Nandia's group was toning in the outer ward. As we made our way through the grid of beds, he told me, "I've never considered that poor copper metabolization could be a complication with Saragalla. I'll put our research people on it and see what they find out."

Father Raphael was with Nandia and adding his voice to those toning. "This is the first sign that Saragalla can be relieved," he said. He looked as if a weight had been lifted from his shoulders. I nodded and asked if he could direct us to our accommodations. Nandia agreed with a weary smile.

We said good night to Sarah and the other children

working with the bedridden. The priest led us outdoors to a small stone cottage behind the church.

As we walked through the night, Nandia said, "Father, we're both exhausted. Would you mind if we postponed our midnight meeting? I was also wondering if we could spend a few minutes reconsidering the idea? Perhaps we could talk more tomorrow?"

The priest readily agreed. Before leaving, he gave us a brief tour of the cottage, pointing out its well-stocked kitchen and two small bedrooms.

I was relieved at the way Nandia had handled our midnight appointment with the black marketeer. Her words didn't seem to trigger any concern that we might have found another source for copper.

I slumped onto a small couch as soon as the door closed. Nandia snuggled next to me to talk.

"Quite a useful day, eh, Bearns?" she lay back against the couch, eyes closed.

"We've still got challenges to settle, but I'm so exhausted I could fall asleep right here," I replied. "What do you say we dowse the causes of Saragalla in the morning, before breakfast?"

"One small problem," she cautioned. "Remember, I gave Dunstan the copper medallions before he left. Assuredly, his adventures could be more dangerous than ours. Hopefully, he'll return to the hospice by breakfast."

"Sounds good." I said, settling deeper into the couch. "I think we may want to separate the two medallions, so we can each wear one. Better yet, if we find more copper, we could make double medallions for the three of us. Just extra insurance against any further disruptions to telepathy or teleporting."

As I heard myself say this, I realized this was just what we needed to maximize our safety. Looking over to see what Nandia thought of the idea, I saw that she had decided to sleep on it.

"Yes, my love, it has been one long day," I said softly. Clambering to my feet, I gathered her up and deposited her on a bed. I draped her with a quilt and turned out the lights.

Lying down in the next room, I was asleep before my eyes closed.

VII

I DREAMT THAT I WAS BEING CHASED by men who were dressed in black and carrying knives. I was terrified, but knew that even in a dream, I could begin connected breathing and heal my fear. My training with Agoragon again proved useful as I remembered that I could alter the direction of a dream simply by choosing a new outcome. I asked the energy within the fear to transform into a desire for a peaceful resolution. Suddenly, my point of view changed, and I knew that these men were no longer my enemies. I turned and faced them, hands wide apart, palms up.

They saw the gesture and stopped running, confusion written across their faces. "Who sent you to do this thing?" I asked.

One man looked directly at me and simply said, "Dashing." Then they both turned and ran away. His answer set me wondering. I was trying to unravel my confusion as the dream faded.

I opened my eyes to a bedroom flooded with sunlight. I was pleased to hear Dunstan and Nandia talking in the kitchen. Eager to greet them, I hurried in to say hello, but my yawning kept interrupting our greetings. Finally Dunstan laughed and said, "Aye, Laddie, you'll be right as rain after some food, don't ya think? How 'bout if I cook?"

I nodded my approval as Nandia poured steaming cups of tea. "I was given a final warning by my flatfoot friend last night," he explained as he cracked eggs into a pan. "From now on, it's open season on us, mates. There's a bloody derry on 'n there's nae a thing anyone can do about it. Orders came from some devil higher on the food chain than even the chief. They even claimed to have misfiled the complaint I had signed against our attackers, so the bastards were set free. And after all the bother I'd gone to tying them to that lamppost so the coppers could find 'em.

"I stopped in at the hospice, hopin' to find you. The priest Raphael proudly showed me that lovely wee lass called Sarah, and the fine work she's doin'. Her fire for healin' is a sacred miracle, so 'tis. Other wee angels followin' her around, singin' new life into that place. We've a worry now about the danger to Sarah and the other blessed bairns. Like wildfire, the news is spreadin' that somethin' miraculous is happenin' at St. Paul's. I've grown quite fond of those wee precious bundles, and asked the good father to have someone he trusts make sure their food's nae bein' tampered with."

Nandia's face drained of color as she listened. We both felt deeply for the lovely ten-year-old whose huge heart led her to want to help people heal. Losing her was something neither of us wished to consider. "We must find out who is pulling the strings here,"

Nandia exclaimed. A strain of worry muted her otherwise lilting voice. "The church could be behind all this. They have the most to lose if their parishioners learn that each individual holds the ultimate authority for their lives."

Dunstan served breakfast and further explained. "There are many factions in Geasa who have investments to lose if this epidemic clears. We'll be needin' more copper if we're to stay one jump ahead of the villains and find the answers we need within the next six days."

Nandia jumped in, "The dowsing work to find Saragalla's causes must be done soon. But not yet. I want to corner Father Raphael. I feel he's the key to learning more about the church's involvement. Dunstan, what else can you do to find the copper we need?"

"I've several friends, Lassie, in high and low places. Prime suspects for squirreling away pieces o' the precious metal." He surprised us with that revelation. "I think it's time to be payin' a visit and collectin' some past due markers. I can't think of a greater need than the one we're facin' right now. About that, me lovelies, there's little doubt."

"Keep your double medallion with you, Dunstan. It'll help in any tight scrapes you may run into," I suggested. "Meanwhile, I need to spend more time at the hospice. I want to see how the severely disturbed cases are doing after my visit yesterday. There's a lot more to learn. Nandia and I can watch each other's backs."

"Aye, you'll be wantin' ta do that, depend on it," our giant troubadour advised. "I've the notion that our good priest is leanin' into the devil's own religion, so he is, decidin' that he's not deservin' o' bein' loved, sad to say."

So, Nandia and I set off for the hospice in search of a priest ashamed of being blackmailed, while Dunstan went to scour his sources for scraps of metal.

VIII

BETWEEN US, AS IT TURNED OUT, Nandia's morning was the more fruitful. After some searching, she found Father Raphael sitting on the floor behind a cupboard in the hospice's scullery, sullen and solitary. He didn't want to talk, but she managed to draw him out. Given Nandia's charm, I doubt this took very long.

"He admitted to feeling guilty, once I'd revealed what I knew about the extortion plot," Nandia later told me over lunch at the cottage. "He also admitted to feeling greatly relieved after we cancelled our meeting with the black marketeer. Our suspicions were correct—Father Raphael had informed his police contacts about our planned meet. So, he blames himself for you getting shot last night.

"After confiding all that to me, he disclosed his greatest shame. He's been photographed in a passionate embrace with Sister Mary-Agnes. They have been in love for years. It's a mystery to him how the photographs landed in the hands of the police. I suspect that someone within the church has links to the underworld and is seeking to discredit him.

"I suggested to Father Raphael that he might just want to expose the extortion plot," Nandia said. "After some discussion, he realized that such a decision could serve the ideals he has for himself, his fiancée and the church. To his credit, his greatest concerns are not for himself, but for the reputations of the church and Sister Mary-Agnes. He's afraid that St. Paul's will be discredited, they'll both be excommunicated and their families publicly humiliated.

"I asked him to imagine the best possible resolution to his dilemma," she continued. "His face lit up when he told me of his dream to marry Sister Mary-Agnes. He has long had the dream that their loving partnership would bring more love into his ministry. Sadly, after receiving those damning photographs in the mail, he abandoned his dream to despair. He was painfully ashamed of how easily he crumbled in the face of the blackmailers' demands and conceded to their terms.

"Fortunately, he was very receptive to receiving healing energy. I worked on his head and his heart as we breathed and toned together. I then talked of how inspired I was to learn of his hopes and dreams. I encouraged him to consider that in some reality, every dream is already true. Then I asked him: If that is what you truly want, why not pursue it?

"It was a completely new idea for him to consider that his desires exist for a constructive reason. He now dreams that the love he shares with Sister Mary-Agnes will prove to be a gift that could change the church.

He was noticeably relieved when I showed him how to transform the energy of his shame into this new direction he sees for the church.

Then, a mysterious gleam of a secret well-hidden flashed across Nandia's eyes. She slowly reached under her cape and withdrew a velvet pouch. "Look at what Father Raphael has been carrying all this time!" Abruptly, she thrust the small, dark bundle into my face, excited as a young girl bestowing a birthday present. Opening it, I was delighted to see two shiny, silver-dollar-sized copper disks.

"He was quite eager to donate them to our cause," she exclaimed. "And quite apologetic for not giving them sooner. It's his gift of gratitude to us!. After our work together this morning, he's revived his passions to marry Sister Mary-Agnes, resolve Geasa's epidemic and transform the church. He has set aside his self-pity and is enthusiastically drafting letters to the archbishop, the Holy Primate and the news media."

We played like children with the copper disks. I flipped one at her, she returned the favor. She tasted hers, I dropped mine down the back of her gown. As we played, the clarity of our original telepathic connection returned. That was the true joy of Father Raphael's gift.

And, while Nandia had been showing the suffering priest the light, I spent the morning working with the most troubled patients, this time with Sarah at my side. She listened intently while I talked with them and administered healing energy. Occasionally, she stepped in to offer her support. While her words weren't as polished as mine, she was a joy to listen to and a delight when toning. It took only a few moments of listening to our harmonies for patients to drift off into a peaceful, rejuvenating sleep.

We fell into a comfortable rhythm. As we moved from bed to bed, the ravings of those we treated slowly stilled. Sometime around mid-morning, Dr. Rosenbloom interrupted our work with some disturbing news.

"Earlier today, the government announced it was awarding a contract to a drug manufacturer to provide a Saragalla vaccine," his voice carried worry. "Yet, our best medical researchers have dismissed the possibility of a vaccine. They say there is no known compound capable of disarming the virus's microscopic hooks that it uses to penetrate cell walls. And, it is imperative that a Saragalla vaccine can disarm those hooks; otherwise, it will very likely accelerate the spread of the disease.

"This news is all the more disturbing since this drug manufacturer is known to have produced dubious vaccinations in the past. There is a well-known case where one of their vaccines, containing microscopic portions of a virus, set off a sudden escalation of the disease they were attempting to remedy. They are known for their fast-and-loose research. And, they have friends in the news media who have published exaggerated stories about the dangers of not treating a disease with vaccinations. Clearly, their intent has been to trigger fear in order to promote sales."

I told him of a similar problem in my homeland. "The government agency responsible for drug approval required that new medications outperform the placebo effect. However, as people grew to understand the power of their consciousness and expand its use, the placebo effect also grew in effectiveness. As the placebo effect grew, the government raised the effectiveness standards for new drugs.

"The drug companies fought the government, in an attempt to remove the higher placebo standards," I continued. "But, they did not succeed. Over time, they found it no longer financially viable to produce new vaccines. As vaccine use declined, the diseases associated with vaccine use declined as well.

"Mind you, this was years after reliable research had demonstrated that the flow of a disease through a population remains unchanged whether or not the population has been vaccinated. Sooner or later, medical science will universally come to accept that the individual is the only entity with the power to assure its own well-being. No one has disease thrust upon them. The only way illness can happen is when we compromise either our self-respect and self-expression, or both.

"All that being said," I concluded, "the government putting out a contract for a Saragalla vaccine is not great news. It's like throwing chum to the sharks. The media is sure to dramatize an entirely new menu of horror stories in their efforts to gain readership. All the more reason for us to push ahead with our work."

"Of course, if I'd known about Father Raphael's copper at that point," I said as an aside to Nandia, "I could have done a better job reassuring Dr. Rosenbloom of our progress toward our Saragalla remedy."

I then resumed the tale of my morning's activities. "After our talk, the doctor was feeling somewhat relieved. As he departed. I decided to check in on the young man whom I'd visited the previous evening. I explained to Sarah the work I had done with him. We arrived to find him sitting on the edge of his bed and showing great signs of improvement. He was happy to see us. He had heard of Sarah's work with her band of children and expressed his heartfelt thanks to us both.

"I wanted to learn more about any emotional problems that had preceded his illness, and asked, "Would you mind telling us what was happening in your life just before you fell sick?"

"I was having trouble with my girlfriend," he replied. "She told me she was interested in someone else. I fell into a pit of depression. I was sure this could have happened only because God was punishing me. I kept telling myself that our breakup was my fault— because I couldn't cut it as a man. I now realize that my ongoing thoughts of self-judgment and feelings of self-loathing had a lot to do with how quickly I fell into the raging stage of Saragalla. I don't know how many days I was trapped there. It was only when I heard you singing to me that I decided I must be worth caring for. That idea helped me understand that I can do a better job of loving myself."

"During his story, Sarah had stepped to his side and taken his hand. "I'm so happy that I was here today with you," she said at the end of his tale. "Do you mind if I tell others your story? What you learned will help them, too."

"The young man happily gave his consent. As I listened to the two talking, I knew that we had to redouble our efforts to teach more people about their tremendous value and power as individuals. This young man could now return home. He had healed himself after only a little help from me. Ultimately, it was his change in attitude from self-punishment to self-respect that had produced this healing.

"At that point, Dr. Rosenbloom stopped by to congratulate the lad. They both agreed that Sarah's presence was uplifting. "It's as if a sunburst just danced through the door," the young man said.

"The doctor asked Sarah if she was ready to begin musically toning in the terminal ward. She was very excited at the request, and ran off to gather the children whom she knew were up to the task.

"By then, I'd grown increasingly more impatient to begin dowsing for the causes of Saragalla. That's when I sent a telepathic message for us to meet for lunch," I said to Nandia. "I was unsure if you had received it, not knowing if our breakfast had supplied enough copper for the telepathic connection I needed hours later. I was thankful to find you here at the cottage."

"Now that I think of it, I did wonder about that mysterious smile of yours when I arrived," I played with one of Father Raphael's copper disks as I spoke.

"It's wonderful hearing of your progress with Sarah and Dr. Rosenbloom, Bearns," Nandia acknowledged, "especially in the terminal ward." She then pulled out her copper disk and her pendulum. "Now, let's explore the causes of Saragalla, shall we?"

We started by affirming aloud that we sought only accurate information from our Inner Selves. We stated our desire to identify the exact causes of Saragalla, and asked our subconscious minds to support impeccable dowsing. Next, we completed twelve alternate-nostril breaths, to cleanse our energy fields of any emotional residues from the past few days. Nandia began dowsing while I took notes. Later, we would reverse our roles to confirm our findings.

Nandia asked her first question: "Is a cause for the Saragalla epidemic an infection?" Her crystal pendulum moved in a vigorous forward and backward swing, her "yes" response.

"Is a cause bacterial?" This time, a side-to-side swing, her pendulum's "no" answer.

"Is a cause fungal?" Again, a side-to-side swing, another "no" response.

"Is a cause viral?" This time, her pendulum's motion changed, swinging forward and back. Nandia's dowsing confirmed what was commonly accepted: that the Saragalla virus was a key to the disease. She pressed on with her questions.

"Aside from the Saragalla virus, are there any other viruses causing this epidemic?"

"No."

"Are any of Saragalla's causes toxins?"

"Yes."

"Metal toxins?"

"Yes."

"Chemical toxins?"

"No."

"Radiation toxins?"

"No."

"Ok, Bearns, we're making progress!" Nandia's excitement was growing. "Identify some toxic metals for me."

"Let's set aside the usual list of aluminum, arsenic, lead, copper, mercury, nickel, graphite, gold, cadmium, and platinum, and instead try zinc, shall we?" My motto is, when in doubt, start with the most obvious question.

We were rewarded with a "Yes." Nandia recalled an earlier comment that zinc toxicities can sometimes mimic copper deficiencies. Some of those symptoms, such as nervous disorders, immune weakness and muscle spasticity match those of the Saragalla disease as well.

Continuing on, we tested for the emotional causes of the epidemic. As suspected, the problem was suppressed fear, as well as the self-degradation that comes from the belief that human nature is inherently evil. We both knew well that such a belief is a major impediment to the expression of individual talents and abilities—in itself, one of the two fundamental causes of any illness.

Nandia and I switched roles. I quickly confirmed her findings. I went on to dowse what percentage of the epidemic could be attributed to each of its four causes. It was interesting to discover that the emotional and mental issues dowsed to be over eighty percent, while the zinc toxicity and viral infection only accounted for a mere twenty percent.

"We will find a way for this society to change its limiting beliefs, Bearns," Nandia affirmed. "People need to accept that individuals are not only beings of good intent, but that each of us is creating our own experience for constructive reasons." While clearly speaking to the heart of the matter, Nandia looked worried.

For several moments, we stood silently troubled. How would our mission ever get accomplished? Nandia worried that a week wasn't much time, while I worried that we had delayed our dowsing far too long.

We began breathing together and suddenly, both of us spontaneously said, "Trust." After a laugh over that synchronicity, we went to work cleaning up our worries. I imagined us as two determined people stomping around and shooing loud, pesky Chihuahuas from the parlors of our minds. Nandia picked up on that image and imagined us using brooms to expedite their departure. Then we spent a moment appreciating what we had accomplished. Our dowsing work was underway and we were getting useful answers.

Then, quite unexpectedly, I recalled a medicinal herb I had used back home. I'd found it helpful for mental and emotional symptoms similar to those of Saragalla. "There's an Australian flower called Angelsword," I excitedly said. "It helps people recover their connection with the Inner Self. If we can find a source of local medicinal herbs, we could test to see if any might serve a similar purpose. If so, we could dowse for its frequency and infuse that vibration into water for people to take ..."

My words trailed off as I puzzled, once again, over how we would solve the problem of finding a radionics instrument.

Eavesdropping again, Nandia nodded and resumed dowsing. She asked her first question silently. Finally she disclosed her findings. "I'm getting that there is a local herb that is an effective treatment for Saragalla's mental and emotional disturbances." She then asked aloud, "Is the same herb also effective in helping the body heal the Saragalla virus?" When her pendulum swung to the affirmative, she exclaimed in delight. "This just confirms what you said earlier, Bearns! Viral infections are held in place by the act of suppressing emotions."

Then, she grew pensive and laid down her pendulum. "It seems to me, Bearns, that within every group, there are some who are naturally skilled at communicating ideas and transmitting energies. I think Sarah and some of the other children fit that description. Once we find the remedy, let's enlist their aid and see how well they reach out to others the community. They may be the answer."

I liked the direction of that idea a lot.

Then, I remembered an earlier unanswered question about toxins causing the Saragalla epidemic. "Give me a second to dowse for a remedy to help with the zinc toxicity," I said. We knew copper remedied Geasa's zinc disruptions to our telepathy and teleportation, but had not confirmed it as an answer for the epidemic's zinc toxicity. I picked up my pendulum and asked, "Will copper neutralize Saragalla's zinc toxicity?" My pendulum swung in a strongly positive direction. Nandia confirmed my answer with her own.

"Well, we can start by providing a copper-rich diet to people at the hospice and monitor the results," she suggested. "So, that leaves us with the immediate problem of finding a medicinal herb that tests as effective for the viral and emotional causes of this disease. We'll need an actual specimen to prepare a vibrational remedy, correct?"

"Right," I replied. "And, I'm wondering if Dr. Rosenbloom or Dunstan might be able to help us find herbs nearby. Let's see if we can mentally connect with our minstrel friend." Another wave of gratitude hit me. Father Raphael's copper was proving to be a sure remedy for my earlier impatience.

We each held a piece of the priest's copper, closed our eyes and imagined Dunstan. I recalled my memory of him playing music, knowing that by visualizing the musician at play, I would improve our mental connection. After only an instant's focusing, Dunstan's craggy face came to mind. His normally playful features were carved into a frown. "In a wee spot of bother here," he indignantly declared. "Could stand with a bit 'o your help."

Our eyes shot open at the same instant. "Let's be away!" Nandia exclaimed. "Hold onto that disk and focus on his face." We grabbed each other's hands and quickly shut our eyes.

I focused on Dunstan's features, reminding myself to inhale deeply through my nose and exhale sharply through my mouth. I quickly completed my teleport protocol and watched as the familiar spiral of white light disappear from within my head. As I opened my eyes, I found us standing in a fetid and slimy rock dungeon, next to Dunstan. He was stooped over, shackled to a post—despondent as a slave hopelessly waiting to be sold at an auction block.

The place was dimly lit from a small window high in a wall, and so rank that, at that moment, the idea of asphyxiation seemed quite attractive. Missing was Dunstan's horn, normally carried in its leather satchel across his back. Upon seeing us arrive, he rewarded us with a broad smile that was followed by a frown of concern as he tilted his head toward the barred door. He telepathed an image of two guards sitting just outside the gloomy chamber.

We telepathically listened to the story of his capture. He sent images of being overcome by four assailants as he left a mountain fastness, home of a longtime friend. We watched as his body was ignominiously searched by the villains who had pinned him to the ground. They stripped him of all his copper and his horn. It happened so quickly that he had no time to call out to us or teleport himself to safety. Obviously, our opponents were getting better at their jobs.

"Aye, the bastards not only managed to nick my double medallion, but a copper ring that I had just been given." He mentally telegraphed hurt, frustration and rage. As he was relaying his story, I liberated my ever-present lock pick from its nest in my belt and made quick work of the locks securing his shackles.

"Why don't Bearns and I wait here while you recover your copper?" Nandia courageously offered her disk to Dunstan, knowing that at least one of us could well be trapped in this hell-hole if he didn't return.

"Aye, Lassie, the element of surprise will most certainly improve me odds." Dunstan quickly took her copper, eager to be away. If he was surprised that we had acquired more of the precious mental, he didn't show it.

"I'll be quicker 'n bonny Jack-the-Nimble, so I shall." With that, his multi-hued energy field faded from view as the sound of his voice trailed him.

Nandia and I found a dry resting spot, out of sight from the door. We mentally planned how to disable the guards, should they decide to check on their prisoner.

With that potential danger taken care of, I asked Nandia, "Did you notice that Dunstan retained enough of his telepathic powers to talk with us from here without any copper? I wonder if the effects of Geasa's zinc deposits are somehow less disruptive here?"

Nandia borrowed my copper and dowsed the question. After receiving a positive response, she continued asking questions to isolate the reason for the change. It turned out that the zinc deposit didn't extend this far from Geasa, although its effects were still strong enough to limit teleportation without copper.

"This could be useful, Bearns," she said. "If needs be, we can always distance ourselves from the city whenever we want to recover our intuitive strength." I was silently considering this nutmeg of solace when Nandia's thoughts suddenly took a turn.

"Why, oh why, does this same old worry keep nagging at me?" she complained. "I would give anything to know why I keep wondering about the monied interests in Geasa opposing its recovery."

More and more, I appreciated Nandia's spontaneous questions. This one triggered a recollection of my dream from the previous evening. "In last night's dream, I was being chased and decided to face my attackers. I turned and peacefully asked who had sent them. Only one word was spoken before the dream faded."

"And? Come on, Bearns, what was the word?"

"Dashing. The word was 'dashing'. It makes absolutely no sense to me."

"Got poor grades in high school French, did we Bearns?" Despite her beauty and grace, there were times when this woman got on my nerves.

"OK, what am I missing?"

"One word for 'dashing' in French is pimpant."

Understanding flooded my awareness. I had been wondering why this dream seemed so obscure, especially since I usually could count on my dreaming for reliable insights.

"That makes perfect sense, doesn't it?" I was excited. "And, since our jeweler friend Pimpant is Raphael's cousin, perhaps the priest can shed some light on the motivations driving Geasa's monied interests."

"And, maybe even explain the origin of these attacks that have been plaguing us," Nandia said thoughtfully.

We were interrupted by Dunstan's return. Triumphantly, he danced a jig, happy as a burglar chancing upon a drawerful of diamonds. He flipped the borrowed copper toward the ceiling, which Nandia deftly snagged mid-air. From the musician's hand dangled the double medallion. A large copper ring graced his ring finger. He had also retrieved his horn and, aside from a bruise darkening his right cheekbone, looked none the worse for wear.

Like true north, Nandia's instincts, again, unerringly guided us. "You wouldn't happen to know where we might find medicinal herbs, would you, Dunstan?" she asked.

"Aye, there's St. Martin's monastery further into the mountains. It has long grown and sold local plants for healing. But let's take leave of this stink-hole first. Just to the east of us lies a thicket o' scrub oak. Shall we crack on?"

He focused on the trees, and reached out for our hands. We tuned into the image he was sending and were next standing in the mottled sunlight of a stand of stunted oaks.

"Aye, we're safe here for the nonce." Dunstan

telepathed. He then gulped a huge breath of relief, like a shipwrecked sailor swimming free of the deep.

"Mind ye," he slowly added, "I suspect that our assailants have telepaths among them. There's no other way the thugs could 'a run me down. I told no one of my intent to visit the mountain, where I met my mate who gave me this ring."

This news was troubling. Suddenly, I felt a surge of impatience to get moving. Irrationally fearful of another attack, I raised my voice to hurry us along.

"Time's awastin', folks. Let's get to St. Martin's!"

But Dunstan urged caution. "Laddie, we've no known friends there. There may be people at the monastery who would feel threatened to learn we've helped St. Paul's hospice. There could be spies for the rascals who seek to pillage Geasa and stall its recovery. Let's find a safe place where we can watch the monastery and take the time we need to collect our thoughts."

As I calmed myself with my breathing, I nodded to the Scotsman. "Festina lente," I heard Agoragon say—Latin for, "Make haste slowly." This was yet another time when I needed to rein in my horses. Once again, we joined hands while Dunstan visualized the entrance to the mountain monastery. We focused on the same image, and in what felt like a whirlwind of light, suddenly found ourselves on a mountain path. It grew wider as it approached a pair of tall, wooden gates.

We quickly dove into the underbrush. Dunstan held a finger to his lips and pointed to a nearby hillside. Its forest would provide the cover we needed while we watched from its elevated position and planned our next moves.

IX

WELL-CONCEALED, perched high on the forested hill, we studied the monastery below. Although alive with activity, its aging buildings had been little cared for in recent years. One wall was beginning to crumble, and several of its roofs needed repair. Most of the monks bustling around were garbed in cassocks worn thin and stitched together like patchwork quilts.

The buildings must have housed over three hundred men. Busily tending to a steady stream of vehicles, they unloaded supplies and filled empty truck beds with bales and crates of herbs.

Luckily, the crush of this frenzy had kept the monks too busy to notice our arrival and scamper uphill. Amidst a cover of bushes, we found sanctuary. It had several peek-a-boo views, and yet rendered us invisible. We watched and talked and rested, remaining hidden throughout the early afternoon. Our deadline, like a dead weight, lay heavily upon my shoulders, but our shared time together lifted some of that burden.

We told Dunstan about Father Raphael's

"conversion" and of our suspicions that Pimpant was one of the leaders in the plot to disrupt our work.

I then mentioned Dr. Rosenbloom's remark about the government awarding a vaccination contract for Saragalla. After some thought, Dunstan found merit in the idea. He suggested we could give the manufacturer our Saragalla herb's vibrational frequency. Then they could produce the remedy.

My mind reeled as I considered the possibilities. The manufacturer also had a distribution system in place. That solved another of our major problems and, hopefully, our remedy would curtail the manufacturer's need to come up with their own chemical cocktail. That option certainly avoided the risk of who-knows-what unwanted side effects a vaccine could have.

I think Nandia enjoyed listening to us for awhile before she brought us back to reality. "If one of the causes for this epidemic is that people refuse to accept authority for their own well-being, then giving them a vaccine that is actually a vibrational remedy seems unworkable on several levels." She continued her explanation with great patience.

"First, we're not being honest with those afflicted about what it is we're offering them. We're treating them as if they're not capable of handling the truth. And second, we are endorsing the vaccine manufacturer, while at the same time turning a blind eye to this deception of its customers. All this, just so we can feel secure that our remedy is being produced and administered to the masses? Are we really prepared to pursue our ideals for Geasa by using means of such questionable value?"

As we listened to Nandia, both Dunstan and I

began to realize the mistakes in our thinking. I know Dunstan certainly had a look of chagrin as we both nodded to Nandia. I'm sure I did as well.

"Sorry." I said. "I was hoping we'd found the answer to at least two of my major worries. I'm afraid I let my anxiety seduce me into justifying a compromised way to reach our goal. So, instead of healing my worries, I let them cloud my thinking."

Dunstan again nodded and thanked Nandia. "'Twas a fine rut I had us headin' into. I'm glad ya were here to shine some much-needed light." Nandia moved to hug both of us when the Scotsman intruded with a raised hand.

"But, I'm wonderin how 'tis that one-third of Geasa's population hasn't contracted Saragalla," he said. "They must have been exposed to the virus. If we study how they think and live, we just might be findin' some helpful clues. It could be more than just a copper-rich diet."

Nandia and I both liked the direction this was going. "Seems to me that we can discover some useful information about how immunity works," Dunstan continued. "I've nae believed that the immune system must fight pathogens in order to restore health. Might it be that immunity is about the body learnin' to communicate with dangerous pathogens to help them contribute to health, rather than cause harm? Why did we get the childhood measles only once? I know there's one thing I'll go bail on—that viruses are no more of evil intent than you or I. We don't know enough about how the law of value fulfillment works in the body as it heals illness."

"Well, no one has ever had any illness or trauma

thrust upon them," Nandia reminded us. "It is only due to the mistaken beliefs of guilt, punishment, blame or self-pity that health crises occur. At some level, healthy people know that they have a choice as to whether their well-being will be violated by a pathogen. I think you're right, Dunstan. We do need to enlist the aid of healthy people to work with the afflicted. That could very well be a way we'll learn something useful." It was only much later that I realized how prophetic Nandia's words had been.

Inspiration lit up Dunstan's face like a sunburst in the middle of a storm. "Ya may not know this, but there are many gangs of adolescents roving in and around the city. Most are wee ones from families torn apart by Saragalla. Starving, they have turned feral and prey on households that have been weakened by the disease. I've heard rumors that while some gangs are dying, others are quite healthy and free from Saragalla. I'd fancy some time with them to learn why. Who knows? We might even be able to enlist their help in ending this epidemic."

Nandia grew visibly excited. "We saw a gang of youthful predators the day of our arrival," she recalled. "Remember, Bearns, that you questioned Geasa's stability after seeing a pack of children roaming like wolves? And, it's suddenly occurring to me, Dunstan, with your musical talent, we could produce a concert for these kids. We could also announce our plans in support of the healing of Saragalla. And, we could invite the gangs to help us reach out to the afflicted, especially those who are house-bound." As her inspiration unfolded, her enthusiasm grew.

Meanwhile, I was growing more and more irritated.

I finally interrupted. "I like the idea, Nandia, but aren't we getting a little ahead of ourselves?"

I was confused, unsure of why I was feeling cranky. Nandia and Dunstan remained silent, waiting for me to say more.

"We need to focus on how we are going to get some Angelsword, not to mention finding its frequency and creating the remedies we need. We have the pressing problem of meeting with Father Raphael and Sister Mary-Agnes. Pimpant's role and motivations in all this need to get figured out, and I'd like to stay at least one jump ahead of whomever it is that wants us out of the picture."

As I spoke, I found myself touching my upper chest, the place where I'd been shot. As I made the gesture, I realized that I had hidden my fears about another attack. My voice rose as my apprehensions grew.

"Now, we're adding to the list a concert for teen survivors and getting feral kids to go door-to-door to homes where people would justifiably be suspicious of them." Despite feeling ashamed of my outburst, an inner nudge urged me on.

"I'm feeling overwhelmed. I can't see how we'll ever be able to accomplish all this. In short, I'm feeling helpless and frightened. We could fail miserably. And, to be painfully honest, I'm feeling damn sorry for myself. Can we please just focus on what we need to do right now?"

Dunstan snorted with impatience and suddenly disappeared. He had obviously decided to take matters into his own hands. Despite her look of surprise, Nandia said three words that were immediately calming: "Trust value fulfillment."

Suddenly, we heard the minstrel's jazzy strands of music rising from the monastery's courtyard below.

"This is one way I believe I'll be able to attract the attention of St. Martin's head abbot," I heard a mental chuckle as Dunstan telepathed his message. "If you'll notice, there are nary a young nor old fair lassie about this place. Nandia's presence could cause us more trouble than we've bargained for. And Laddie, I'm glad ya got what ya were needin' ta say off your chest."

Nandia and I smiled at each other as we watched the musician playing his horn and dancing his jig. As in the city, it was his enthusiasm that made his performance infectious. A gathering crowd encircled him as more and more monks stopped to listen. Others began emerging from within the monastery, curious about the unusual music they were hearing.

He played on as a small group of somber-looking monks approached. They surrounded an elder cleric who wore a faded red robe, with brighter patches at its elbows and hem.

The elder stepped forward and interrupted Dunstan with words we could not understand. We did recognize, however, his welcoming gestures. We mentally heard the Scotsman say that he hoped to enlist the monastery's aid to help eradicate the Saragalla epidemic. I sensed he was concerned that his sudden arrival might arouse suspicion, and, therefore, was unwilling to reveal our presence.

Several of the monks shook Dunstan's hand. Surrounding him, the group then escorted him into the building. Only then, did the courtyard's flurry of activity slowly resume as monks reluctantly returned to their tasks. Many faces were shadowed in disappointment—their rare moment of entertainment cut short.

We maintained our telepathic rapport with Dunstan. He acknowledged our mental presence and provided an ongoing commentary on his progress through the building.

At one point, the three of us heard a new voice telepathically urging caution. "Take care with your thoughts; not all here wish you good fortune in your endeavors."

We couldn't tell who had sent the warning. I wondered if it was the elder monk who had greeted Dunstan, or perhaps a member of his entourage. Whoever it was, they were friendly enough to warn us of the possibility of danger nearby.

I found it quite a challenge to still my thoughts to keep from revealing our presence to an unfriendly telepath. I pictured my mind as a peaceful pond and breathed deeply through the maddening temptations of wanting to think, talk, shout and scream with impatience. I did have to admit, though, that I was feeling much calmer since my outburst earlier.

Nandia and I watched the images Dunstan sent as the group made its way deeper within the confines of the monastery.

Its interior was in better repair than its deteriorating outer shell. A central passageway was flanked by high stone walls, interspersed with alcoves that were home to a variety of religious artworks. Among the statues were shepherds wielding tall crooked staffs alongside paintings of broad-winged angels protecting young children. Youthful acolytes scurried to sweep floors and tend torches, preparing the way for the oncoming delegation. At one point, Dunstan telepathed a brief view of a small chapel off to one side, where a few aged monks knelt in front of a candlelit stone altar.

As they came to a pair of dark-stained, heavy wooden doors, we heard Dunstan ask, "Is it possible to meet with the monastery's senior monk to discuss herbal preparations for the Saragalla epidemic?" As if guided by some unseen hand, the dark doors swung open. Dunstan was ushered into a spacious workspace. Its stone walls were lined with herb-covered tables, its floors accented with thick, colorful, woven carpets. Narrow windows framed leaded glass that cast bands of amber light across the floor. An acolyte had just begun lighting the first of the room's many candles.

An aged monk wearing an oft-mended robe stepped forward to greet the troubadour. As tall as Dunstan, he extended his hand in welcome. Beneath a thick mane of snow-white hair was a kind face, chiseled by ages of warmth and wisdom.

There was a cast to his dark eyes that struck me as somehow familiar, yet before I could explore that impression, I heard him say, "Welcome, minstrel. It has been many years since our courtyards have been graced with the pleasure of such delightful music. I am the senior priest here at St. Martin's, known simply as The Abbot. I pray I find a way to return the favor of your performance." As I listened to his voice, I realized then that it was his telepathic message that had earlier urged caution.

Dunstan immediately warmed to this man and took time to introduce himself. He told of having been ma-rooned here on Fantibo, and spoke longingly of his desire to return to his Scottish home. I was surprised to hear him disclose that he, too, was a Grand Council delegate. He told The Abbot about Nandia and me, and revealed that we were anxious to meet him.

Finally, Dunstan explained that we had discovered that copper resolved the disruptions to telepathy and teleportation that were being caused by Geasa's zinc deposits. This information seemed to delight The Abbot, who noted that he had encountered the same difficulties whenever travelling to Geasa, but until today, had not known their cause.

"And, am I to understand," The Abbot smiled, "that you've arrived here hoping to find answers to the Saragalla epidemic?"

Dunstan returned his smile and nodded in agreement. He then asked The Abbot for permission to include us in the conversation.

"By all means," exclaimed the priest. "I will happily accommodate anyone who counts themselves as one of your allies."

Dunstan telepathed to us, "Come now. It is safe!"

Nandia and I clasped hands, mentally focused on his face, breathed deeply and arrived.

Our troubadour introduced us to The Abbot, who said, "We don't often get visitors to St. Martin's who travel so efficiently. Perhaps I can assist in your quest to find an herb that can help rid Geasa of its epidemic."

Pride showed in his deeply lined face as he turned to tables that were laden with dried plants. "These are all the medicinal herbs that we are currently using. As far as we know, none of these remedy Saragalla. But, perhaps you know of a way to prepare or combine them that will prove to be beneficial."

"Thank you, Father," Nandia replied. "Bearns and I are skilled at pendulum dowsing and would like to test your supply of herbs. There may well be combinations that will work. We also seek the means to translate herbal essences into electromagnetic frequencies. A radionics instrument would be most useful."

"These herbs are at your disposal," The Abbot graciously replied. "And, I may be able to help with your other needs as well. However, I must warn you that there are monks among us in the pay of those who seek to profit from this epidemic. I suspect that some of them are capable telepaths. Please recognize that the danger to you is very real if you are either seen or heard here."

I reminded myself to guard my thoughts and rely only on my spoken words to convey my ideas.

"May we dowse to see if any of the herbs here will answer?" I asked.

Stepping back, The Abbot swept his hand toward the tables. Nandia and I began to dowse each plant. It took only a few minutes to determine that none of the herbs present were effective for our needs. I asked if using them in combination would benefit, and again received a negative response. I then dowsed to see if another local herb would be useful. To that question, I received a positive response.

I then turned to The Abbot and asked, "Father, do you know of any other medicinal herbs growing in this area?"

He nodded enthusiastically. "Indeed there are, although none located conveniently nearby. A remote valley among the mountains to our north grows many species we have yet to study. The valley is at least twenty miles distant. We've carved a rough track with our hard-travel vehicles, so we no longer need to walk or ride mules to get there. I am happy to locate it for you on a map. Your teleportation skills will allow you to arrive there without detection. But not today. As you see, it already grows dark."

The Abbot pointed to a window, where the last of the daylight was fading.

"I can provide a safe haven here for your night's rest. But, I strongly suggest you set out before daybreak. The less curiosity you arouse, the better."

A group of younger monks arrived to shunt tables aside and erect three sleeping cots. From deep within the monastery, a bell rang, marking the evensong benediction. The Abbot joined us as we sat in silence, enjoying cups of warm tea and listening to the beautiful, resonant harmonies that are so characteristic of a practiced male choir. My body gradually settled into a state of deep peace, a child-like trust in my oneness with all of life. It was the same feeling I remembered from my childhood visits to church. My worries gently melted away. Working together, my body and mind settled into a sense of love and reassurance that emanated from my deepest, inner core.

As the chanting and hymns ended, we were served a simple meal of a thick, vegetable stew with a dark, homemade bread. Its aroma was divine.

We quietly talked with The Abbot about our progress to date. Our trust in him grew. Nandia related the tale of Father Raphael's entanglement in the extortion plot, as well as his passion to revolutionize the church.

The Abbot was eager to discuss needed changes for the church. "The majority of clerics throughout this galactic sector ardently support an end to the vows of poverty and chastity," he said. "They are tired of not being trusted and are hungry for a dogma that recognizes the sacredness of humankind rather than its sinfulness. Father Raphael can certainly count on St. Martin's support. Please pass that message along to him at your earliest opportunity."

Before retiring, The Abbot produced a map and pointed out the valley we were to explore in the morning. We memorized its position in the mountainous region to the north. Dunstan and Nandia agreed with me that it would be wisest to travel together.

Exhausted, we were about to bed down, when we were delayed by The Abbot. "Before you retire," he said mysteriously, "there is something I think you'll be interested in seeing."

He directed us to follow him across the room, where, sweeping aside a curtain, he revealed a cupboard containing several radionics instruments and their related paraphernalia. I whooped for joy.

"These were given to the monastery decades ago, in repayment for a small service we were able to render to an outworld trader. Since then, the abbots of St. Martin's have known little about this equipment, other than it can be used to produce safe, non-toxic, energetic remedies. None of us has ever learned how to operate these devices. I believe they will be useful to your cause."

"What a stroke of good fortune!" I exclaimed. Beside myself, I eagerly examined the equipment. I started with an instrument with which I was familiar. It was a decades-old model, built to last. Its rheostats were all calibrated from zero to nine and powered by two quartz crystals. Because of its independent power source, I dismissed the other instruments in The Abbot's closet.

The instrument had an output well that would only accommodate a hundred-milliliter bottle, therefore making sufficient volume of our remedy a time-consuming process. Then again, it was equipped with potency and intensity dials, so we could make solutions at higher concentrations than needed. These could then be diluted, which would speed up production. I was happy to see a stick plate, a feature that easily enables dowsing for accurate frequencies. So now, it would be a breeze to determine all the frequencies we needed to remedy Saragalla.

"This will do nicely." I was well pleased. "Now, we must find a safe place to produce our remedies, in the volume Geasa needs. We'll also need hundreds of liters of distilled water and thousands of sterilized glass bottles. Abbot, do you know of where we might secure those supplies?"

The Abbot nodded. "We have an abundant stock of the supplies you need," he said. But, again, he cautioned us, "Here at St. Martin's, gossip races like a fire before a stiff wind. By now, word of your mission is surely pulsing through the grapevine. It will not be safe for you to work here without the risk of sabotage.

"That said," he continued, "If your herb-hunting expedition is successful, we can prepare large amounts of its tincture. That could well be a boon to many who are suffering."

I greatly appreciated The Abbot's generous offers. Despite the note of apology in his voice for the forces there that opposed our cause, I knew he was telling us that we needed to find another place from which to produce and distribute our remedies. That was tomorrow's problem.

It had been a very long and productive day. We wished The Abbot a peaceful sleep, and in return, he offered blessed dreams. As the monk departed, Dunstan settled into the cot nearest an open window.

"I'm knackered, so I am," he said. "As this day began, I wouldn't have guessed that we would find an ample supply of copper, the radionics gear we need and be planning a mountain expedition. I like how we work together. Sweet dreams of healing, me lovelies."

His sentiments echoed mine. I looked over to Nandia, who was already snuggling in under rough blankets. "And ask for dreams that lead us to the herbs we need," she smiled. With that, I was left alone to dream my dreams of Nandia.

X

THE ABBOT'S RETURN awakened us just before dawn. Three acolytes followed him, carrying trays of steaming porridge and tea. The distant sound of morning prayers being sung accompanied our otherwise silent breakfast. We looked over the map one final time, after which The Abbot said, "Godspeed. I pray for your safe return, laden with all the herbs you need."

"I don't know how we can ever repay your generosity," I replied, "but I hope to find a way." My two companions echoed similar sentiments.

Then, after a reminder from Nandia to concentrate on the valley, the three of us clasped hands and whisked away.

We arrived amidst a scene of breathtaking beauty. Warming a clearing sky, the sun dismissed wisps of clouds that were reflecting the last rays of sunrise. The valley was surrounded by tall peaks sprouting carpets of fir trees that thinned near timberline. Reminded of the mountains of home, I found myself wondering when next I might walk those familiar hills. For a moment, my heart ached. Then, as I breathed in the cool air, I found comfort in the scent of pine and wildflower sweetness. In the near distance, I could make out a marshland, water lapping at its edges.

"Those plants growing near the water look promising," I suggested. We set off in that direction. We followed a narrow animal trail that was overgrown in spots, often stopping to enjoy the spectacular views of the surrounding snow-capped peaks. At the water's edge, I invited my companions to sit with me on a hillock of grassland that overlooked the marsh.

For a time, we sat in silence, breathing in the cool, fresh, mountain air. The smiling face of my maternal grandmother settled in my consciousness. Then I heard a quiet whisper, as she offered to help us find the herb we sought.

"My maternal grandmother was a Cherokee Indian," I said as I yielded to an impulse to talk of her wisdom. "It was her teaching that nurtured my childhood passion to master the use of energy. It was she who first taught me that thoughts always follow energy. She taught that thoughts are powerful, creative acts. She said that our thoughts touch all of life at some level of the subconscious. She helped me learn that we are all telepathic, and the best way to send an idea to someone is to imagine them engaged in a familiar action as you send your message. Best of all, she taught me to listen."

I went on to tell Nandia and Dunstan of the Native American teaching of the four directions of the Medicine Wheel.

"To each of the cardinal directions was ascribed a

human power," I said. "To the North, the energy of the Earth, belongs the power to listen and to speak. To the East, the energy of Air, comes the power to know and to know that we know. In the South, the energy of Fire, reigns the power to use our power, while the West, the Water energy, holds the power to feel and the power to heal.

"And so, Grandmother set me on the path of learning the incredible power of the individual. 'Try having one of your giant corporations grow an arm or a leg,' she used to say. 'It's only the individual that has such power.' Her teachings of the Medicine Wheel laid the framework for my refusal to accept degradation and lack of respect for any individual's path.

"She helped me learn to listen to plants sing. This was an ancient tribal ritual used to find the best herb for an ailment. She said to walk through the woods musically toning. Then after a few moments, mentally focus on the specific illness to be healed. Begin nurturing a peaceful sense of inner listening. In this way, I learned to hear each plant as it sang its own unique song.

"As I grew in my ability to listen to nature in this way, I gradually was able to identify which plant sang the loudest. That was the herb most useful in healing the illness I'd identified.

"Today, let's each wander around this wetland," I said to Nandia and Dunstan. "I wish you great joy as you find your own connections with this valley. Listen to the plants. Mark the loudest and bring a sprig of that plant back with you. We'll meet back here again when the time is right."

"Aye, Laddie, I do envy your blessings," said Dunstan. "To have been born with such a hallowed gran. Do thank her for me."

We parted company. I set out along the western edge of the marsh, thinking of Saragalla's symptoms and listening as I walked. For a while, I was distracted as frogs leapt out of my path and turtles lumbered away. The day grew warmer. I shed my jacket and sat along the water's edge. Breathing deeply, I relaxed, laid back and felt my body absorbing the energies of the valley. A deep tightness I'd been holding about the success of our journey melted away. "Nature absorbs emotion," I heard Agoragon's words in my mind. I re-awakened to an inner knowing that I belong to nature as much as each mountain does. I was imagining the entire day spent in this reverie of peace until suddenly, I mentally heard Dunstan's rough brogue: "Get crackin, Laddie!"

Laughing at his prod, I stood up and resumed my search. I found my senses were heightened as I continued along the waters edge. I began toning as colors became brighter, mountains sharper, sounds clearer. Listening, I could easily hear the songs of each plant I passed. I refocused my mind's eye on the Saragalla symptoms. It wasn't long before I mentally heard one song repeating itself, clearer and louder than any of the others. Following that music, I was drawn to a broad-leafed plant adorned in purple blossoms. Shaped like an inverted fleur-de-lis, each flower proudly displayed a bright yellow stamen.

Dowsing confirmed that this plant would be an effective treatment for Saragalla. I asked which part of the plant would be most useful and was surprised to find that the leaves, rather than roots or blossoms., tested positive. I gathered up several handfuls from a number of plants and headed back to our meeting place. I enjoyed my heightened sensitivities and, together with a covey of small flying and crawling creatures, lazily explored in the beauty of flowers blooming along the way.

Nandia was already there, waiting. I was pleased to see that she held a bouquet of the same herb that had sung to me. She was breathing in its aroma with a look of delight on her face.

"Your grandmother's method of selecting herbs is quite effective," she said. "It seemed that I felt her presence during my search. After I heard this plant singing and gathered its leaves, she spoke to me."

"Oh???"

"Yes, she asked if I would help you overcome your appetite for bad jokes. She must have been quite a wise woman." She laughed at that.

"That sounds just like something my grandmother would say," I soberly said. "I sincerely hope neither one of you slips on a banana peel after doubting the quality of my humor."

Ignoring that bad joke, Nandia again smelled the bouquet of leaves she held. "I've never seen anything quite like this species," she said. "Do you know what it is?"

I examined the herb in my hand. "It appears similar to Angelsword back home. The important thing is that it sang to both of us. Now, I wonder what Dunstan foun ... ?"

A shout arose from a nearby hillside. There, descending toward us, was a group of at least two dozen adolescents, led by the flamboyant Scotsman. They were laughing and teasing each other, happily heading our way. In his hand, Dunstan carried the same herb Nandia and I had identified. Several youngsters in the group also carried bundles of the plant.

"You'll never guess, Laddie, who I found chewing on the very herb that happened to be singin' to me." He laughed infectiously, obviously pleased with his newfound friends. "Remember how we were wonderin' how 'twas that some gangs seemed immune to Saragalla? Well, I think we've found the answer. These young folk ran across this selfsame herb some time ago and discovered that it keeps them healthy. They come here whenever they need to harvest more, and they've begun to share it with others! It only took a wee bit o' convincin' to get 'em to see the wisdom 'a workin' with us."

"Hey, Mister," called out a taller boy from the back of the crowd, "Dunstan promised us that we could still sell this plant to other groups. Is that right?"

"We can do even better than that," Nandia replied, one jump ahead of me. "How would you like to help eradicate Saragalla, and find a home to return to as well?"

"That sounds a lot better than sleeping in the rain," a younger girl responded, one of the few females in the gang.

Even though they were unkempt, they all looked healthy and quite capable of taking care of themselves. As they gathered around, introductions were made. I then asked how they came to discover the herb.

"I heard an angel singing about it in a dream," a girl called Cynthia said. "We were hiding in these mountains from a gang of sickies. All they want to do is hurt people. Anyway, while we were hiding, the angel sang to me about this valley. None of us has been sick since we began chewing the leaves of Angelsong, as we call it."

"That sounds like a very good name. Do you mind if we adopt it?" I asked. They happily agreed. I invited them to join us. "We could certainly use your help back in Geasa. We want to use Angelsong to make a remedy for the Saragalla epidemic. We need plenty of people to deliver the remedies to hospitals, hospices and the sick who are housebound. Like Nandia said, we'll find a way to make sure you're taken care of and, hopefully, even find new homes for you. As you're probably aware, many families have lost children, and many children have lost parents. I'm sure there are people who would love to welcome you into their homes, especially when more people learn that Saragalla is not incurable."

Dunstan impatiently hurried us along. "We'd best be crackin' on, Laddie. It'll take a day for us to get to St. Martin's. Hopefully, there we'll find rides to get this mob to Geasa.

"The good news is," he said, "turns out these rascals can carry a tune. I imagine with a bit 'o coaching, they'll be able to hold a decent harmony by the time we get to the city. I reckon a vagabond choir is just the thing to open our concert.

"'Twill be a grand way to introduce the Saragalla remedies to other homeless groups and the city at large." As Dunstan expanded on Nandia's earlier ideas, his excitement grew. "Once again, I've been praisin' the Good Lord that Nandia is here with us. But to do this thing, Laddie, you'll need get to St. Paul's hospice ahead of us. Find anyone there who can travel easily. We'll be needin' lots 'o help spreadin' the news of the concert. And, you'll have to be right sprightly makin' enough of your remedies to go 'round."

I was pleased with Dunstan's ideas. These kids had shown us a way to deliver an answer to the epidemic!

Nandia danced up to Dunstan and gave him a big hug. "I do hope you'll be teaching them some decent songs," she teased. "Not any of those bawdy numbers you like to sing when you think no one's listening."

"And I suppose you'll be wantin' to hike with us back to the monastery, just to make sure we'll be usin' your approved song list." His eyes sparkled as he taunted her in return.

"As a matter of fact, mister, that's another first-rate idea," she gaily replied.

It was obvious that Nandia relished the thought of spending time with these young people. In turn, they had warmly welcomed her into their group. "I can tell them more about our remedies for Saragalla," she firmly declared, "And save them from having to wade through your usual malarkey."

"Then I'm away," I said loud enough for everyone to hear. "I must find a way to transport remedy equipment to a safe place in the city. I'm so pleased to have you joining us. I will find a way to put on your concert the evening of your arrival. I trust, Dunstan, that you'll be up to your usual inspiring performance as well?"

"Aye, happy to, Lad. Just make sure you stay one jump ahead o' the reptiles on the way, and don't forget to call if you're needin' any help."

It was reassuring to know that we were in telepathic rapport, regardless of our different paths. I focused on

The Abbot's sanctuary, breathed, and with the familiar spiral of light in my head, found myself next to his herb-laden tables. My sudden appearance startled him as he sat writing at his desk.

"I don't know if I'll ever get used to these arrivals of yours, Bernard, but it's wonderful to see you again." His face clouded over with worry. "But where are Nandia and Dunstan? Has there been some trouble?"

I quickly reassured him that they were doing well, and related the tale of our discovery of Angelsong. He grew quite excited when I told him of our most important find—the gang of children who had originally discovered the herb.

"Dunstan and Nandia are bringing them here. I expect they'll arrive sometime tomorrow. Father, these youngsters have been selling the herb to other groups of displaced kids, all of whom appear to be quite healthy."

I showed The Abbot the handful of the herb I had brought back. He was quite pleased to learn how effective it could be.

"Why don't I send several of our hard-travel vehicles up to collect the group?" he suggested. "That should cut their return time in half. And, with your permission, I'll make arrangements to have you all transported into Geasa as well."

I was thrilled to accept his offer and nodded in agreement. He then continued. "And since there's no need to spend time trekking, why not ask your group to gather up a generous supply of Angelsong? That way, we can get started producing its tincture. Check in with your friends while I get the transports on their way."

I interrupted his departure by asking, "Father, might you be able to provide packs or crates for teleporting the radionics gear to Geasa?"

"Easily done," he replied. "And please allow us to donate the remedy bottles and distilled water you need." He left and I puzzled over the question of where to deliver these supplies.

As I considered St. Paul's, I was suddenly distracted by my appreciation for The Abbot's compassion and generosity. His quick thinking had just solved two of our most pressing problems. I imagined his white mane and chiseled face, and telepathed a message of heartfelt gratitude. I felt quite humbled at the sudden good fortune this priest had bestowed upon us.

Then I recalled his concern that telepathic messages could very likely be overheard by those unfriendly to our cause. I considered the problem and realized I had to take the risk. It was imperative that Nandia and Dunstan know of The Abbot's gracious offer of transport and supplies. There was no other way to accomplish what was needed in the time remaining.

At that moment, Agoragon's image came to mind and I heard him say, "If you want to secure a telepathic message, just imagine it enfolded in a loving caress of white light." I found myself smiling at that wisdom.

I spent the next moments breathing and forming a mental picture of Nandia and Dunstan in front of me. I visualized them in the act of picking Angelsong, remembering what Grandmother had taught: "Take the time to imagine your target in motion. It will be much easier for them to tune into your message."

Then, I used Agoragon's white light suggestion and telepathed, "The Abbot is sending a ride to collect the group. This means you'll be back here by nightfall. He's offered to produce the Angelsong tincture. Can you collect enough of the herb so the monastery can make it in quantity?"

"Aye, with the help of these vagabonds," Dunstan reassured me. "We'll easily gather more than we need."

Then I asked, "Nandia, can you join me? I need help transporting the radionics gear to our cottage in the city."

"... Be right there," she answered.

I sent her an image of The Abbot's quarters and knew she would be arriving soon. Then, I began spreading out all the radionics components that had been stored these many years. As I worked, a new worry emerged: The gear I wanted took up over half the floor space.

"Our arms will be more than full moving all that." Nandia's voice surprised me. I hadn't noticed her arrival—being preoccupied in a debate with myself over which pieces of equipment I could leave behind.

"It's good to see you," I said, distracted. After a quick hug, we went straight to work.

"I'm deciding what we can do without and stacking only what we need next to that doorway." I pointed to the pile of equipment I'd settled on taking. "How much do you think you can carry comfortably?"

Nandia began lifting boxes and said, "I can teleport maybe two, maybe three fairly light boxes at a time. But, if my attention gets distracted by the weight, I'll be unable to move." Silently, she shook her head. "Bearns, haven't you learned that ancient adage, 'Heavy loads take many trips'? Why not call in Dunstan, too? I'm sure you've heard the one, 'Many hands make light work.'"

She was right. After quickly checking to confirm that Dunstan was on his way, Nandia began arranging the collection of boxes going to Geasa into smaller piles. Humming a lovely tune, she bent to the task with a lightheartedness I so admired. She had that enviable quality of bringing happiness and ease to whatever she was doing.

Obviously eavesdropping again, she interrupted her tune with a simple phrase, "Trust the present."

"Thank you, M'lady," I said, and returned to my task of selecting components. Suddenly, a loud shriek pierced the air. I turned to see Nandia suddenly drop the box she was carrying and dive under the nearest table.

"What's wrong?" I blurted.

She was pointing at the box she had dropped, eyes wide with terror. I stepped toward it and saw a large, hairy spider scampering out of sight.

"Bearns," she shouted, overwhelmed by her fear, "KILL IT!"

"You mean the spi ..."

"Yep, terror! Need your help."

My eyes immediately led me to a broom in a corner. I hurried over, grabbed it and positioned it so the spider could attach itself to its bristles. As the critter advanced toward my closest hand, I deftly grabbed the broom's opposite end. Then I pointed the handle toward Nandia. Mentally tuning into the spider, I asked if it would assist us with some healing.

"I'm pleased that you would even consider such a request, Human," it telepathically responded. "I'm doubly pleased that you are of no harmful intent. Those are such rare qualities among you two-leggeds these days. Of course, I will be of assistance in whatever way I can." I sensed a decidedly feminine personality.

"Nandia, are you willing to let this spider support you in healing your fear?" I asked gently. "And, by the way, I think it's a girl."

"Pardon me, Buster," the spider mentally interrupted. "But that would be 'Ms. Eight Legs' to you."

"My apologies. I do stand corrected," I telepathed.

Then, I said to Nandia, "Actually, the spider prefers to be called Ms. Eight Legs. Would you like her support?"

"Maybe. But can you keep Ms. Legs away from me?" Her voice was shrill, eyes growing in terror as the spider advanced in her direction.

"No problem." I kept a gentle tone in my voice as I reversed the direction of the broom by shifting the placement of my hands. Legs traveled first one way down its handle, and then the other. Hopefully, if Nandia could watch Ms. Legs and me at play, she would come to see the furry creature as a being of good intent.

So, as my dance with the spider continued, I decided to tell a South American wisdom-tale, often used when children encounter monsters in their dreams. Nandia indicated that she was open to hearing this story, provided I took care to keep Ms. Legs at a safe distance. After agreeing, I said, "Indigenous tribes often tell this monster story when teaching their children to face their fears."

Nandia began breathing deeply, her eyes focused intently upon the spider who was dancing along the broom.

"First, a child is instructed to watch for monster sightings in their dreams," I said, as I continued reversing the broom. "They are told it is perfectly natural to have fears when spotting a monster. It's also perfectly natural to run away. However, the child is instructed to stay close enough so that it does not lose sight of the monster, while making sure to keep a safe distance. From this vantage point, the child is then directed to watch for the moment when the monster shows its teeth. Upon seeing the monster's teeth, the children are told to take a deep breath and show the monster their own teeth—and it doesn't matter if it is a smile, a song or a scream—just make sure the monster sees their teeth."

"Once the monster has seen the child's teeth, the child can then ask the monster any question they want. For, once the monster sees the child's teeth, it is required to answer all questions truthfully.

"Of course, there is only one question that everyone wants to ask a monster, and that is, "Are you here for my greater good?" If the answer is 'No,' then the child automatically has the power to dismiss the monster. After all, it's seen the child's teeth, and must comply with that child's wishes. But, if the monster answers 'Yes,' then the child can ask for whatever gift, wisdom or awareness the monster has to share. It will gladly present its gifts, for that is its obvious purpose for being in the dream.

"After thanking the monster, the child is told to remember the dream and share it with their family upon awakening. In this way, children learn that facing fear is much more effective than hiding, hysterics or trying to fight it. And, they learn that facing fear is a path that benefits the entire tribe.

"Nandia," I concluded, "the next time Ms. Legs advances toward you, watch for her teeth." I knew the spider had been listening and trusted her to cooperate. "Remember, the moment you see her teeth, show her your own." Nandia's eyes grew even bigger with fear. With great intensity, she watched Ms. Legs approach. Suddenly, despite her terror, Nandia opened her mouth, yelled and flashed her own teeth. And, at that moment, she began to relax.

I have been impressed with this woman's attributes many times. Yet, it was the courage she displayed as she watched Ms. Legs dancing toward her that impressed me the most.

"Bearns, remind me again of the question," she asked.

"Is she here for your greater good?"

"Riiiight."

Nandia concentrated on the question and, as she asked it, the tightness that edged her face began to drain away. "I'm remembering the time in the third grade when a spider landed on my shoulder," with trembling voice, she relived the incident. "I screamed and ran out of the classroom. Had I been chased by the devil, I could not have been more terrified. For years afterward, I was ridiculed as a coward for my lack of courage. I felt so ashamed that I just wanted to die." At that, Nandia burst into tears.

I began breathing deeply, knowing that this was a healing of a long-buried pain. Certainly from childhood, and, quite possibly, a previous life. Gradually, her breathing began to mirror mine and Nandia resumed talking.

"During my tears, Ms. Eight Legs spoke to me," she said. "She asked me to consider that I've been withholding love from the frightened child part of myself who was taunted for being afraid. She reminded me that I could help that fearful child accept herself as a universally beloved individual. She is free to work on any lesson, at any time. Neither fear, shame nor any other emotion has ever compromised that fact.

"Legs also said that the attacks I suffered as a child were never thrust upon me. The only attacks I've ever experienced were by my invitation only, to help me see the distortions in my own thinking. With my innate power to hold myself above violation, it is my choices alone that shape my well-being. At the moment I realized that others' attacks were reflections of my own self-diminishment, all of my terror disappeared."

"Nice work, Nandia," I said. Deeply touched, I knew that I had just witnessed a sacred moment. I restrained the urge to take her into my arms. After all, Ms. Legs was still perched on the broom in my hands.

Then, Nandia cautiously stepped toward me, her hand outstretched. "Please, may I hold Ms. Legs?" she asked tentatively. Slowly, she further extended her hand. The spider softly hopped onto her palm. Nandia's eyes widened again. Then, she carefully raised her hand, bringing Ms. Legs to eye level. "Thank you, Dear Ms. Spider Friend," she said. "I will always remember the great service you've done for me today." Side-by-side, Nandia and I then walked toward a nearby window, where she extended her hand out into the open air. Ms. Legs rappelled down a web-strand to a bush below. "Dear Friend, thank you for your assistance," I telepathed as she landed softly.

"It was a rare pleasure indeed," she replied. "Be assured I shall be telling the tale of this day to countless numbers of my children." She then presented us with a brisk, two-arm salute and disappeared into the foliage.

Without a word, I turned to face Nandia. We warmly embraced. The merging of our energies was at once electric and magnetic. We reveled in those energies for a time, before I said, "It was more than wonderful to watch you face your fear, my love. You have so often helped me heal mine. From you, I've learned to trust that I create only those events that fulfill my individual and our collective values. Something tells me that you'll be sharing the tale of Ms. Legs many times with many others."

Nandia took my hands, looked into my eyes and said with deep gratitude, "Bearns, I'm warmed by your caring and warmed by my love for you. I wouldn't have missed this journey with you for any world. And won't it be fun remembering that we'll always have Legs?"

The image of the furry spider came suddenly to mind. I heard a high-pitched chittering, and realized it was Ms. Legs, telepathically joining us in our laughter. As our shared gaiety faded, the spider's image also began to fade. She telepathed her last words, "And I will always have you two, as well." Then, Ms. Legs was gone.

It was a day I'd not soon forget.

Looking into Nandia's aura, I could see that the colors in her energy field were now brighter and more vibrant. Suddenly, in the midst of this renewed vitality, she loudly snapped her fingers. "You know, Bearns, an idea was germinating when Legs first appeared," she exclaimed. "Now, I'm convinced it's a very good plan. I think I should let myself get captured the next time we're attacked. That way, I can make my way to the head of whatever snake so venomously opposes us. Once there, I can discover if our suspicions about Pimpant are true."

Just as I was about to protest, there was a shimmer in the air and Dunstan unexpectedly appeared in the doorway. Obviously, he had been listening and began voicing his objections before I could get a word in edgewise.

"Aye, Lassie, and just what kind of men would we be, to let such a tender moment as you take that kind o' risk? There's got to be a better way.""

Listen, you two," Nandia's said sternly, "if by now you don't trust my ability to take care of myself, you're too many whistles short of a tune. We've enough copper to make this work. I could also be wearing your ring, Dunstan, while hiding my disk safely on my body. If need be, I'll let them take the ring, but I'd still be able to stay in touch and escape if necessary. That way, you'll know if I land in a jam and need your help. I know full well that you'll both be there if I need you."

Sometime during this exchange, The Abbot had returned. He was carrying several empty crates. I could see from his aura that he was reluctant to meddle in the affair, yet was favoring Nandia's planned adventure.

As for Nandia, I knew that the more she talked about the idea, the more determined she would become to follow through with it. I decided to steer the conversation away from our problems with Pimpant and asked, "Dunstan, do you think you can abandon the troupe long enough to help us get this radionics gear to the hospice?"

"Aye, Laddie, but I'll need t'be gettin' back before The Abbot's trucks arrive. Our rascals are collectin' all the Angelsong they can find."

Then, he turned to Nandia and asked, "Lassie, can I trust ya'll nae dash off on this wild goose chase o' yours 'till we've talked more about it?"

While a flash of doubt crossed Nandia's face, she quickly softened and said, "I know you both have my best interests at heart. So, yes, I'll not set out on my own until we've had more chance to consider the idea. Meanwhile, let's get this gear to the cottage in Geasa. I'm getting another of my impulse-feelings that now would be a good time to talk with Sister Mary-Agnes."

XI

IT TOOK JUST TWO TRIPS to teleport the radionics equipment to our cottage. I remained behind with The Abbot, making arrangements for remedy bottles and distilled water to be delivered to the hospice.

The Abbot was ready to produce the Angelsong tincture, once the herb reached St. Martin's. Without delay, it would be shipped to Geasa. I agreed to send a case of our radionic remedy back to the monastery, with dosage instructions.

I mentally connected with Nandia and Dunstan again and asked if they could teleport a day's supply of bottles and water back to Geasa. That job took two more trips. The rest of the supplies could arrive in The Abbot's trucks with the musician and his band of young ruffians.

In a hurry to return to the valley, Dunstan quickly bade us farewell. Nandia and I teleported to St. Paul's, seeking out Father Raphael and Sister Mary-Agnes. We found them in an empty vestibule of the church locked in an embrace that would have otherwise been a very private moment.

The red-faced Father Raphael quickly recovered and said, "Mary-Agnes, I'm pleased that you finally get to meet Nandia and Bearns." He warmly introduced us, despite his embarrassment of being caught kissing his beloved. Nandia and the nun immediately hugged, as if they'd known each other for years. I was delighted to see that the two women looked so alike they could have been sisters.

Then, turning to me, Sister Mary-Agnes graced me with a warm hug. "We are so thankful for all that you've done to help us end this epidemic," she said. "But, could you please tell us how we can ever repay you?"

"Well, Sister, that's easy," I answered. "I've been hoping that you might help us create the remedies we need." I then explained our plans for the creation of the Angelsong remedy using the radionics instrument.

I wanted only trained, competent people producing the remedies. That way, Nandia, Dunstan and I would be free to make whatever peace we could with our hidden adversaries. We were growing weary of their repeated attempts to clip our wings.

"I need half a dozen nuns who have been trained as nurses," I continued. "In a few hours, we want to have bottles sterilized and the production of remedies under way. We need a roomy, secure location. Is there one close by?"

"Oh, yes," the nun said, brightly smiling. "And, if I may say so, I'm just the person for the job." She looked around at each of us, making sure there was no objection before continuing.

"We have an empty dorm in the convent next door that can easily be converted to your needs. And, I've already spoken to our few remaining nuns. We all would love to help in any way we can."

Nandia thanked Sister Mary-Agnes with another hug. She then turned to the priest and asked, "So, Father, how go your plans to revolutionize the church?"

"Leaps and bounds," came his enthusiastic reply. "Happily, Mary-Agnes said 'yes' to my marriage proposal. The local news media has agreed to cover the wedding. With that kind of publicity, we hope there will be enough favorable public opinion to at least delay the church's usual excommunication inquest.

"For my sermon this Sunday, I'm taking on the devil guilt and its brother, original sin. I want to explain that within each person's soul lies the certain knowledge that punishment for mistakes and failings is a flawed idea. It smothers the joy out of growth and brings it to a standstill."

The priest lovingly put his arm around his fiancé's waist. "We've got a big job ahead of us. We're going to help people discover that we are all sacred beings living in a loving universe.

"I now know that my path is to teach that every person's true passion is to express their greatest fulfillment. An artist's true joy lies in creating works that inspire. A teacher is inspired when students grow to discover the treasures deep within themselves. Clerics yearn to encourage each of their flock to accept authority for their own lives. I want to build this church on the ideal that each individual is an excellent, loving creature. And, I believe that resolving this Saragalla epidemic will be a powerful catalyst for transforming St. Paul's!"

"It is quite inspiring to hear you so passionately express your ideals, Father," Nandia said warmly. As they had listened to the priest, both women were beaming with pride. They blessed him with a three-way hug.

Nandia then told the story of our discovery of Angelsong, and of Dunstan bringing gangs of homeless children together for the upcoming concert.

Father Raphael interrupted, excited, "I hope I'm able to announce Sunday's sermon at the concert. It would be my first opportunity to spread the idea of original innocence."

Nandia informed him that Dunstan had been telepathically eavesdropping, and that he heartily endorsed such an announcement.

I wanted Sister Mary-Agnes to hear more about our plans, "We would like to test our electromagnetic remedies here at the hospice. If they're as effective as I trust they will be, we'll need to quickly distribute remedy bottles throughout the city. We want to enlist the aid of homeless gangs. Our plan is to have them go door-to-door, handing out the remedy to as many homes as possible. None of us will be surprised if some of these young people find homes for themselves as they tour Geasa's neighborhoods."

The idea of whole new families being created sparked a great sense of wonder and awe—as if we'd just witnessed some long-forgotten comet crossing the night's sky.

I hated to intrude on the moment, but pressed on to move our plans forward. Turning to Father Raphael,

I asked, "Would you happen to know if any of the children who are helping out at the hospice were previously gang members?"

But, the priest seemed to be lost in thought. Sister Mary-Agnes responded in his stead. "There must be at least twenty-five youngsters who fit that description, Bearns, each one inspired by Sarah's work. They have been learning deep breathing and vocal toning. The children's program is working so well that many patients have returned to their homes.

"Shall I assume," she then asked, "that you'd like me to inform these young people that we want them to return to their gangs and enlist their aid?" After I nodded, she happily continued, "They'll jump at the chance. One thing I can say about each of them is that they're hungry to find ways to do more."

Breaking out of his reverie, Father Raphael's eyes suddenly lit up. "I think I can convince St. Paul's powers-that-be to hold the concert here. While several of our elder priests might oppose the idea, with the excitement that's erupting over these miraculous healings, I think I can diffuse that problem. The cathedral can hold up to a thousand people. A concert could very well galvanize Geasa's recovery from this epidemic. At the same time, it will build a wonderful foundation upon which to build a new church." The priest's enthusiasm was infectious. We were all grinning like Cheshire cats, pleased at how our plans for the concert were taking shape.

Sister Mary-Agnes grabbed my hand and tugged, "Come, Bearns, let's get you and your equipment to the convent. Raphael, can you send a group of trusted guards to help us?"

She readily took command of setting up the radionics lab. In what seemed like mere minutes, Nandia and I had inserted a spray of Angelsong into the instrument and used its stick plate to determine the herb's frequency. Then, the radionics instrument was used to transfer that frequency into dozens of sterilized bottles that were filled with distilled water.

On a whim, I tested with my pendulum to see if the frequency I recalled for resolving problems with copper metabolization would be beneficial. I received a positive response and found that both frequencies could be combined within a single remedy bottle. It took only moments to show Nandia and the group of nuns how to operate the radionics instrument to imbue both frequencies into each bottle. Within the hour, there were over sixty bottles of the Saragalla remedy ready to be delivered to the hospice.

As I finished showing the nuns how to label bottles with dosage instructions, Nandia drew me aside. She was eager to confer with Dunstan, and wanted his support with her plan to infiltrate our adversary's inner sanctum. With my growing respect for her resourcefulness, I found myself warming to the idea. I had to agree, it was time to settle the matter. We stood together, clasped hands and telepathically tuned into Dunstan's energy.

As the familiar feeling of the flamboyant musician's vitality washed over us, we were instantly in touch with him. His natural optimism was a calming balm for the frenetic pace of the day.

"Once again, Laddie," he quipped, "I'll drop in to ease your sufferin'. I trust you've talked Nandia out of her crazy idea to steal her way into the lion's den?"

"I'm reconsidering," I replied. "The idea does have merit, and like Nandia said, we can trust her to reach out for help. Should trouble find her, we can well cover her back. Let's get together and talk more about it."

"Aye, Lad, if there's one thing you're dead right about, it's that we do need to get together," he replied. "If only to talk about how you and I would feel if Nandia's plan goes sour. That said, for too long, we've milfissed the balfastards. 'Tis time to bring an end to their nasty tricks, of that I'm sure.

"Nandia, I'm nae crackin' hardy over the risks you'll face if we go through with this. If we do go through with yer crazy idea, we'd best be honin' contingency plans, if ever we need ta be pullin' yer pretty fat from the fire. And then, I want a contingency plan to back up our contingency plan. Can ya hold off bein a sacrificial lamb till then?"

She readily agreed and presented a new question to Dunstan.

"Sister Mary-Agnes tells us there's a number of gang youths who are recovering nicely and now helping Sarah with toning and breathing. We could use their help to enlist other gangs for remedy distribution. But, I've been wondering if some from your mob want to help with that chore? And, who knows, you may find that a few of these city urchins can add some decent harmonies to your songs."

"I'm nae idiot, y'know," Dunstan teased. "I've been listenin' as you've been lollygagging about. A few of these bonny nubbins know how to get to some a' the city gangs. And all o' them are keen on the idea of helpin' out with remedies and even more keen to be findin' new families. There's nary a solitary one who doesn't jump at the chance. My problem is, I need a couple of hours to get there. We're only just arrived at St. Martin's. I'm needin' to get this clan, as well as all the gear you need, settled into trucks and on the way."

We decided to finalize the contingency plans for Nandia's capture the very first moment we could all get together at the hospice. Meanwhile, it was time to test our Saragalla remedy. Nandia, Sister Mary-Agnes and I each grabbed a case of remedies and set out for the hospice across the courtyard. We chattered away like jays about a brighter future for so many lost children. Our excitement grew as we then considered the city's prospects for recovery—bigger families, more jobs, greater prosperity and a reborn church.

Unfortunately, our joy and enthusiasm blinded us to our surroundings. Our usual, practiced caution had whistled away with the wind. Quite suddenly, we found ourselves beset from all sides by a band of at least a dozen determined assailants. It was as if they had appeared from out of thin air.

I mentally called for Dunstan's help as I threw my case of remedies at a nearby group of three grim-looking thugs. One went down, the other two got well drenched while fending off a shower of broken glass. I dove into a roll and came up in the middle of another trio.

Nandia jumped in front of Sister Mary-Agnes, her arms and legs flashing in rapid succession. She was doing a damn fine job of putting men down against overwhelming odds. I crashed two thugs' heads together and settled a third with strong elbow jab to his kidney. I quickly spun around to face another attacker, as three cutthroats grabbed me from behind.

They slammed me to the ground—hard. That knocked the wind out of me, leaving them ample opportunity to immobilize me. As the biggest of the trio savagely jammed his knee into my spine, I realized that they weren't interested in inflicting any damage—they merely wanted to take me out of the action.

Feeling helpless and suddenly fearful, I watched from the ground as a pack of four jackals surrounded Nandia. The cowards threw a net over her body. Two of them picked her up and spirited her away at exactly the moment Dunstan arrived. By then, I had recovered my breath and was free to regain my footing. Several stragglers stayed behind, half-heartedly sparring with Dunstan and me. Once they realized that Nandia was beyond our reach, they bolted with the rest, making good their escape.

And so, Nandia disappeared.

Enraged, both Dunstan and I stared at each other with stunned looks of failure and loss. We were mired in silent shock until we heard Nandia mentally sing, "Well boys, it looks as though these toughs have made our decision for us. Stand down for awhile and let's see where this abduction leads." That set off a wave of loud, vitriolic condemnation.

"Gawddam those dog-hearted flap-dragons to bloody hell," Dunstan cursed.

"Double goddam," I loudly swore. "Those canker-ous, lily-livered bastards." Fear for Nandia's safety throbbed through my entire torso.

"An' no one there to watch the lassie's back—should'a ne'er left you two alone. Blast it." Dunstan threw his hat onto the ground and stomped on it.

Our vehemence raged unabated until we were,

once again, interrupted by Nandia. "Your worry for my safety is touching, boys, but remember, I will call upon you at the first sign of trouble. My copper is well hidden on my body, so I'm quite capable of teleporting from danger whenever I wish. Stop worrying. I'm signing off now in case there are eavesdroppers, but keep me informed of your progress. Now, get another set of remedies to the hospice and take care of our sweet sister."

Her message did little to placate us. We'd heard it all before. Dunstan and I fumed and cursed and stomped around like two spewing four-year-olds on a Christmas Eve—after learning that Santa's reindeer had gone missing.

Finally, an exasperated Sister Mary-Agnes cut in. "Gentlemen, how long is this tantrum going to last? No one is hurt. Those boys obviously wanted only to kidnap Nandia, not hurt her. Don't you think we might want to consider why this has happened, and what our options are?"

Checking an impulse to lash out, I realized this nun was right. I connected my breaths and found that my anger was hiding a deeper fear of feeling ashamed. I asked Dunstan if he was feeling the same way. He nodded, and acknowledged his feelings of despair and powerlessness. Then, an image of Nandia's face intruded. Breathing deeply, she winked at me. "Emotional honesty—that's the ticket," she telepathed. She reminded me again that all of my thoughts and feelings are creative playthings.

The breathing helped calm me. I told myself to trust that even this was part of the inevitable flow of value fulfillment.

I turned to Sister Mary-Agnes and said, "My apologies, Sister. I'm just angry that I feel so weak and ashamed. But, your question helped. I'm now ready to look at my hurts as messengers." Breathing again, I let myself locate and feel my hurt feelings.

"I can see that I need to change the thoughts causing this pain." I breathed again and slowly admitted that I was feeling childishly silly for believing that my value as a man was somehow at stake here.

"It's a hurt that goes back to my childhood," I revealed. Both Dunstan and Sister Mary-Agnes were listening intently. "As the eldest son of my family, I came to believe that protecting my siblings affirmed my strength and masculinity. I tried to avoid feeling weak or vulnerable out of respect for my father, whom I greatly admired. One of my greatest fears was failing at my job as the elder brother. Even more, I feared failing to be a good man.

"The most embarrassing part right now is that I know that these beliefs about manhood are a trap. I thought good men were supposed to protect people from getting hurt. That burdens me with the attitude that those I'm trying protect are not fully capable, powerful beings, creating their own hurts, healing them and growing in the process. So, I'm sorry to say, that what I've believed to be a noble cause, has, instead, left me anticipating weakness in others.

"But I know that none of us is a victim," I concluded. "We each have more than we need to attend to our own individual well-being. As a result of what I'm learning at the moment, I would much rather use the power of my manhood to help others discover their own power to hold themselves above violation."

A smiling Sister Mary-Agnes stepped up and tenderly hugged me.

Dunstan chuckled and added, "Aye, 'tis a fine speech, Laddie, so 'tis. You've topped that one well for both of us. Many's the time I've fought and hurt others rather than admit that I was trying to prove my manhood. Thanks for letting me ride along for that lesson."

I imagined Nandia's face and mentally hummed a note of appreciation for her strength and support. Another huge weight had lifted from within. Healing my feelings of fear and powerlessness was, obviously, much more useful than trying to prove I was a good man.

Nandia's face came to life, her eyes lit up and I heard her say, "Glad you could use my help, Bearns. It's always nice to see grown men accepting more of their true creative power."

"Aye, ya helped me ken an important lesson, as well, Lass," Dunstan added. "I see my tryin' to protect ya' has been a problem. For that, I am sorely sorry. You've every right to expect that we use our energies constructively, toward useful outcomes.

"And, now that I think of it, I'd lief be a fly on the wall watchin' ya play the contrite schoolgirl with those henchmen who've nabbed ya. Now, there's a sight we'll nae see every day." The three of us had a good laugh over that picture, and then warmly said our goodbyes.

Dunstan, Sister Mary-Agnes and I returned to the convent to gather fresh cases of the Saragalla remedy. As we walked toward the hospice, Dunstan wondered aloud about the motive for Nandia's capture. Sister Mary-Agnes suggested that their reasons most probably weren't ransom but, more likely, another extortion attempt to waylay our progress. That made sense to me, too, especially since the thugs could now threaten us with harm to Nandia. I sincerely hoped that her abduction was nothing more than a villainous desire to grind our plans to a halt by taking her out of the picture.

Suddenly, Dunstan remembered that there were people at St. Martin's who awaited his return. Setting his three cases of remedy bottles near the hospice door, he disappeared behind a wave of farewell, a worried smile and the fading shimmer of his colorful aura.

Sister Mary-Agnes and I finished delivering the remedies to the hospice. I explained dosages to Dr. Rosenbloom. "Let's begin with fifteen drops, three times a day. If symptoms suddenly exacerbate, it's the body's signal to reduce the dosage.

"There's absolutely no risk of side effects," I reassured him. "After all, we're dealing with distilled water which is carrying electromagnetic frequencies."

The doctor was eager to begin, and gathered Sarah and her choir of singers to distribute the bottles. We explained dosages to the youngsters and answered their questions. Then, I announced that we needed their help with tomorrow's concert. "We simply need more of you young people. Those of you who have been with gangs, can you visit them and invite the other members? We need more help distributing Saragalla remedies at the concert, and if they can sing, all the better." Like hungry young pups bounding at their kennel gate, these kids were eager to do whatever they could to help Geasa's recovery. With that energy alone, the city couldn't help but reclaim its health.

A beaming Sarah came up to me. "Bearns, many people who were here two days ago have gone home. Sister Mary-Agnes told us about your remedies and we can't wait to see how they work. I'm hoping those who are still here will recover even faster."

Clearly, helping people heal had been good medicine for Sarah. She had grown so vibrant and alive that I felt like I was in the presence a fledgling, balanced on the edge of its nest, ready to attempt its first flight.

She talked of Dunstan's choir and asked, "Is there a way we can also be part of the singing?"

I felt like I'd rather get shot again than let this girl down. I mentally tuned into Dunstan and asked him to listen in. Then I said to Sarah, "Let's see if Dunstan can get here to teach you his repertoire of songs."

"Aye, I've been truly inspired by that bonny lassie's gifts, so I have." His message was steeped in enthusiasm and warmth for Sarah. "That very first night she learned musical toning proved to me that she's a rare one with a great heart. Tell her to gather any of the others who want to sing. I'll make sure that they are well rehearsed before the concert."

I passed along the musician's message. Then, accompanied by several nuns, Sister Mary-Agnes and Sarah, I set out to see how well our remedy would work.

XII

THE DAY EVOLVED into a progression of moving from bed to bed, one ward to the next. I made sure both helpers and patients understood how to take their remedies. Most patients had done surprisingly well at putting Saragalla's characteristic symptom of hopelessness behind them. They reported that the children's musical toning had restored their trust in their ability to heal.

At times, I worried about Nandia, but found some comfort in knowing she was tuning into my thoughts. I took her mental silence as a sign she was being cautious about sending messages. I worked on trusting that we would hear from her if a need arose.

Sister Mary-Agnes was busy helping both the nuns at the radionics instrument and those preparing copper-rich foods. Cases of bottles filled with the Saragalla remedy were being stockpiled in storerooms. Nuns, with a group of teens in tow, set out to distribute cases to other hospices around the city.

Dunstan got in touch and let me know that five

trucks, carrying three gangs of youths and the rest of our supplies, were headed for Geasa. I set aside the question of how the gregarious Scotsman had gathered more gangs, and telepathically watched his convoy raising rooster tails of dust as they traversed dirt tracks and mountain passes. Memorable scenes of alpine forest beauty were followed by lofty spires of dark red rock, sculpted eons ago by the wind and rain. As the day wore on, I caught glimpses of the trucks speeding along paved roads, moving at a very good clip.

By mid-afternoon, I had nearly completed my rounds at the hospice. I spent some extra time in the terminal ward giving out remedies, as well as healing energy and toning for the most difficult cases. Sister Mary-Agnes brought a new case of bottles. She laughed with delight as we discovered she had a natural talent for musical toning.

My energy was flagging, so I turned over the few remaining patients to her. Just as I was about to leave for the cottage, a note of alarm was telepathed from Dunstan. "We're needin' your quick mind again, Laddie. Trouble."

He projected an image of the highway ahead of him, blocked by countless police cars and vans. Red and white lights were flashing like an over-decorated Christmas tree.

"Hold that image, Dunstan," I said, and began breathing deeply. I quickly teleported next to the truck that stood at the head of the convoy. The minstrel unfolded himself from its front seat, greeted me warmly and then gave a nod toward the garish police presence.

"They've announced that we're all under arrest

for attempting to foment civil disobedience," he said, scowling at the raucous blaring of sirens up ahead. "Clearly, these fiends 're followin' some senior demon's instructions, hopin' to intimidate us. We've nae said a word."

After a moment's inner listening, an idea began to blossom. "Why not let them take us to Geasa?" I chuckled, realizing this could work in our favor. "At the very least, we'll be saving The Abbot some fuel."

Dunstan smiled at me. "Aye, I do like how your mind works, Laddie." His eyes glimmered as he realized that the strategy would, at the very least, give us more options. "And, up until now, all I could imagine was days behind bars, pacing like a caged animal. Gawd, how I hate dungeons."

"I don't know why, Dunstan, but I'm getting the distinct impression we're about to have some fun," I said. I was feeling a decided sense of optimism about this caper. Although my outer, rational mind had already begun dueling with a cloud of doubt, I simply decided to doubt my doubts—just ignore them.

Dunstan walked back to reassure the group and line them up along the curb. I headed for the lead police car. There, a senior officer was holding a bullhorn.

Calmly, I approached and said, "Officer, my name is Bernard. No one in our group is carrying weapons." I wanted to assure him that we were cooperating fully. "We'll need your help in getting all of our group into your vans. While we're loading, might I inquire as to why we are being arrested?"

The officer smiled at me, visibly relieved that he could accomplish his ends without the need for force. He turned toward the fleet of police vehicles, where dozens of officers, weapons at the ready, were crouched behind open doors.

"Stand down," he shouted through the bullhorn.

His men holstered their weapons, looking relieved. He then turned back to me and announced, "My name is Captain Krepkie. I've been ordered to transport you to police headquarters in Geasa, where you will be processed and held until a magistrate can hear your case. The charges against you range from assault, petty larceny and burglary, to fomenting civil unrest."

"Thank you, Captain." I said. "Which van would you like us to begin loading?"

I wanted the group underway as quickly as possible. The concert was tomorrow! Every minute here was a minute away from completing its necessary ground-work, rehearsing choirs and dispensing remedies. I banished my Nandia worries to the back caverns of my mind.

Returning to our convoy, I watched Dunstan moving down the line of young people, teasing one here and telling a joke to another there. Occasionally, someone protested against the police action, but Dunstan buoyed up their flagging spirits. Combining his usual vitality and confident good humor, he would shake a hand or lay a comforting palm to a shoulder. Rattled emotions were soothed, ruffled feathers were smoothed. To one young girl who was troubled by the siege, he suggested several favorable outcomes for her to imagine.

As I signaled our group to begin moving toward the vans, I stepped in at the head of the line, exchanging introductions with the young people nearby. Up ahead, Captain Krepkie was directing his officers to form a double cordon on either side of the open doors of the nearest vehicle.

As we drew near this cordon, a plan finally crystallized in my mind. I quietly passed along the idea to the youngsters around me. "Just before getting into the vans," I said, "I want you to look directly at each police officer, and loudly greet anyone you know. Pass the word."

It seemed highly likely that some of the youths would be related to, or at least acquainted with, some of the police. I wanted to take advantage of those relationships. I was curious to see just how many police would recognize youngsters as lost family, friends or neighbors.

I didn't have long to wait. "Uncle Todd!" yelled out the second in line, a tall, gangling sprout with wild hair and torn clothes. "It's me, Aaron!"

A young officer tentatively waved from the cordon as a look of disbelief shot across his face. "Aaron? We'd given you up for dead!"

"Hey, I'm very much alive," Aaron grinned, and spontaneously embraced his uncle, despite the shotgun the man cradled.

Other shouts arose from Dunstan's gang. Some were questions, others shrieks of recognition. "Franklin," yelled another youth, and quickly, a second officer and a lad were hugging each other.

Police who had lost loved ones to the ravages of Saragalla began moving through the ragtag bunch, looking closely at faces. "Grandpa?" shouted one gleeful girl, and a graying trooper whooped in return. A young policeman loudly shouted, "Emileeee!" and a young girl raced toward him, screaming, "Daddy! Daddy!"

The mob of homeless youths was now running toward the police, while the discipline of the cordon dissolved. One officer grabbed a tall boy, asking, "Tyler, is that you?" But the boy, embarrassed, pulled away. "Sorry sir, but my name is Riley, Riley Ambrose. I'm very sorry."

There was disappointment on some faces, but the reunions continued. Krepkie's orderly plan for loading police vans had now devolved into the hue and cry of a very disorganized chaos.

I heard Dunstan telepath, "Take care of Krepkie; I'll mind this mob."

The Scotsman bustled the last of his group toward the melee as I stepped out of the crowd to make my way toward the captain.

"I apologize, Captain, for this unruly behavior." I was smiling broadly, as was he.

"This isn't going to look very good in my report," he laughed, obviously not that worried in the face of so many reunions. "I lost a son to Saragalla, and wish that every one of my people could be reunited with someone they've lost."

"I'm here to help Geasa clear up this epidemic," I said. "We're just beginning to distribute an herbal treatment that was discovered by this mob of outlaws. They've been selling the herb to help other gangs, while trying to stay one jump ahead of a hostile group. With the remedy we've developed, it looks like the disease can be completely eliminated."

"I've been hearing rumors of miracle healings at St. Paul's," Krepkie remarked. "Something about singing and hands-on energy healing, which I dismissed as malarkey. Is that some of your doing?"

I confirmed that what he'd heard was true. Then, I took the time to tell him of Nandia, Sarah and the raging young man who had been strapped to his bed in the terminal ward. "As he was recovering, he told me of losing the love of his life," I explained. "He helped us discover that emotional disturbances aggravate Saragalla's symptoms. Father Raphael of St. Paul's is bringing the church in to help with that problem."

I went on to talk about our concert and our plan to enlist the gangs' aid to spread the remedy across the city. "We've been hoping that these homeless kids could find new families. We plan to announce the idea as they sing at the concert and distribute remedies. That colorful Scotsman in the kilt over there has been molding this mob into a choir," I concluded.

Krepkie gazed thoughtfully at the disorder caused by the growing number of reunions. After a few moments, he appeared to have reached a decision. "I'm expected to report in to the chief of police by day's end," he said. "I think we can, without creating any undue alarm, extend this operation for another day. We can use these vehicles to transport these kids and your remedies to neighborhoods around the city."

I restrained my urge to hug Krepkie, concerned that such a move could be misinterpreted and undermine his position of authority.

The excitement of many reunions began to turn into talk of family news and reminiscences. Some policemen, whose families were missing children, began asking unattached gang members about lost loved ones. And, we overheard talk of creating foster homes for the orphans. Some gang members were hesitant about that idea, yet the overall mood was one of joyful celebration.

Krepkie announced to his men that he was revising the operation. He asked those officers who had recovered a lost child to sit with their foundlings in the first three vans.

As the vehicles filled, we counted twenty-two successful reunions, leaving thirty youths still on their own. This second group was loaded into a waiting bus, where Krepkie, Dunstan and I occupied the front seats.

While settling in, Dunstan suddenly swore, "Oh, good Lord in heaven, where's me mind? Captain, a small matter we must attend."

"We've provisions that are still aboard our trucks that we're needin' to make our remedies," he explained. "I've surely drawn the crow for forgettin' 'bout 'em till now."

"Not a problem," Krepkie laughed. "And let's leave that crow behind." He quickly directed his officers to form a bucket line between The Abbot's trucks and the police vehicles. Everyone piled out of their vans and buses. It was a rare sight indeed to watch uniformed officers working side-by-side with ragtag gang members, passing crates and boxes from hand to hand. The two groups began bantering, youngsters teasing police as officers ribbed youngsters. I telepathically thanked Dunstan for remembering the supplies when he did, and asked him to explain later what the hell a crow had to do with it. It took only minutes for the bucket line to finish the job. After reloading ourselves into our assigned vehicles, our new convoy set out.

Our bus resonated with raucousness as we rode toward Geasa. Looking happily relieved, Dunstan expertly practiced the group in their repertoire of songs.

It occurred to me to ask Krepkie's opinion about reaching out to Geasa's other gangs. "Captain, what do you say to using this mob here to scour the city and invite even the feral gangs to join the concert and help distribute remedies?" I asked.

"What a terrific idea," he exclaimed. He was visibly relieved. His excitement grew as he continued, "You may have just come up with the very way to mend the rift between Geasa and its homeless gangs. It's been a plague on my mind worrying how to re-weave that torn fabric of our community. Do you work this well when you're not under arrest, Bernard?" We shared a chuckle over that question.

We were silently enjoying the passing landscapes when my curiosity, once again, got the better of me. Cautiously, I turned to the Captain and asked, "By the way, Sir, was I one of those charged with assault?"

He laughed and said, "Most assuredly. Several of our off-duty officers identified you as the person who had violently interrupted several attempts to arrest you."

"And, did one of your gentlemen happen to shoot me during a scuffle?"

"Yes," he replied, suddenly chagrined. "And for that, I sincerely apologize. We heard rumors that you had healed from that wound within hours. It was then that several of my officers began saying that something unusual was afoot. As a result of that single event, a number of us began to quietly question whether the departmental position was true—that you were not acting in Geasa's best interests."

I had hoped that my quick healing would have caused a stir, and was pleased to hear Krepkie confirm that it had. I then realized that I was feeling less fearful and more at peace with having had a bullet go through my body. Clearly, the law of value fulfillment was at work.

The vehicles slowed as we came into Geasa. Excited to be returning to the city, youngsters began pointing out familiar landmarks to each other. A short time later, we pulled up in front of St. Paul's. Dunstan went looking for Sister Mary-Agnes to arrange a rehearsal for his ever-growing choir. One of the parish nuns appeared and began passing out leaflets for the concert. Krepkie and I organized officers and youngsters to deliver cartons of remedies, printed instructions and concert flyers to nearby neighborhoods. A number of young people told us they knew how to contact other homeless gangs roaming around Geasa. Accompanied by more of Krepkie's men, that group, with concert flyers in hand, set out to spread the news.

A troubled-looking Dunstan joined me as the last of the vehicles departed. Despite the joy of the day's reunions, both of us were still troubled that we knew so little of Nandia's dilemma. Yes, our trust in her had grown, yet, our worries had little abated during the intervening hours.

The troubadour pulled me aside and removed his copper medallions. I liked his idea—without the metal it would be more difficult for our adversaries to eavesdrop on our thoughts. Now was a good time to use Geasa's zinc deposits to our advantage. I removed the disk I was carrying. We hid them in the cottage and began a walk through the streets. Talking in low voices, we brainstormed strategies for finding Nandia.

"We could try breaking into Pimpant's jewelry store, in the hopes of finding at least a clue as to where she's being held," I said. But I was only grasping at straws.

"Aye, the selfsame thought crossed me own mind," Dunstan admitted. "But that straw's pretty thin at the moment, so 'tis. We've your pimpant dream, which I admit, 'tis a solid clue. And I've always been suspicious about the way Pimpant pointed you in the direction of Father Raphael. It's a sure bet he knew his cousin was hobnobbin' with the bobbies. Could be he's a telepath. Seems to me the blighter is ayeweys tryin' to cruel your pitch—since the very beginning.

"So, if Nandia is, in fact, in Pimpant's clutches," he concluded, "I pray she'll think to pinch his copper supply. At least then, the lass could communicate with us safely," he sighed. "T'would be a rare moment, so t'would, when I've felt more frustrated at nae knowin' what ta do."

As twilight fell, we were still unsure of our next moves. I considered asking for police assistance and said, "We could report Nandia missing, get another high-level brush-off, and very probably compromise Krepkie's position."

"Not bloody likely," was Dunstan's laughing reply.

So, we wandered on and found ourselves drawn to the heart of the city. There, we unobtrusively walked past The Opulatum.

The shop was dark. No one was moving in or outside the store. We sat in a nearby cafe, watching its entrance long past the time when night overtook the streets. Still, we were none the wiser than when we had first begun. Finally, Dunstan stood up and said, "Let's at least get some rest, Laddie; tomorrow's chockers, to be sure. I've got to muster bevies of the wee ones for their warblin' at the concert. We'd best plan on a large crowd."

As we drew near St. Paul's, we could see Sister Mary-Agnes frantically waving an envelope over her head as she stood beneath the hospice porch light. Shaking her head with impatience, she brusquely reported that the note had been delivered by a feral gang. Inside was a quick note from Nandia, written on the back of a napkin. "Take care, Pimpant is our man and can tele-path," I read out loud. "Dream together tonight that we find a way to resolve his anger and fear. I'll be with you tomorrow. I'm OK. N."

The cryptic note gave no clue for the reasons behind Nandia's kidnapping. It did, however, explain how our attackers knew of our plans. Dunstan and I talked of what might have befallen her since that last fateful moment when we watched her net-shrouded body being spirited away. He wondered how she managed to get her note into the hands of a roaming gang. Thankfully, her message confirmed that it was Pimpant who was behind the sabotage of Geasa's recovery. And, most importantly, we now knew that Nandia was alive and well and would be with us tomorrow.

Dunstan began talking about what he knew of the power of dreaming. "There's a tale in my homeland," he told us, "of a time thousands of years past when tribes settled wars by collectively dreaming of a battle. The following morning, the dream victor was declared the winner of the conflict and asserted his right to lay claim to its spoils. Entire regions changed hands as a result of dream battles. As this practice spread, fewer warriors were killed in battle. More were taught effective dreaming. Nandia must have picked up that I've been trained in this art. Count on the lass to come up with dreaming as a way to deal with Pimpant."

Agoragon, as well, had insisted that I learn to use this power. I knew that if we focused our collective energies on the night's dreaming, we could very well create a solution to Nandia's abduction. And, we might just find out what was behind Pimpant's need to undermine Geasa's recovery.

"Let's make sure we wear our copper while sleeping," I suggested. "It could well help us make clearer choices during our dreaming."

Sister Mary-Agnes nodded and related how valuable she had found her own dream work. "For years now, I've been keeping a dream journal and am amazed at how often I realize solutions to problems once I've awakened. It really works!" She then turned the conversation to the day's events at the hospice.

"I'm hearing good news from the nuns and young people who are handing out remedies." she said. "So many spirits have been lifted just hearing that there's an answer to the epidemic. Most have heard stories about Sarah's band of healers and their musical toning. In the morning, let's send her out with her students to teach toning and take remedies to other hospices around the city."

"Aye, 'tis a fine thing that the momentum for healing Geasa's epidemic grows, so 'tis," said Dunstan. "Ne'er let it be said that one fine lassie daesna change the world. But. let's take care to have a couple a' Krepkie's men tag along."

All at once, a trio of nuns hustled through the

hospice doors, interrupting our conversation. They herded the three of us inside and then began fussing to make sure we were warm and well fed. Both Dunstan and I had forgotten to eat and ravenously wolfed down two servings of vegetable stew and fresh salad. Like a bird, Sister Mary-Agnes nibbled a bit and then flew off to check on Father Raphael's preparations for tomorrow's concert.

Returning to the cottage, Dunstan and I brainstormed dreaming ideas. We had twin objectives—to assure Nandia's safety and pacify Pimpant and his minions. We knew that the vibrations of our voices would seed these desired outcomes. Exhausted, we lay down and quickly descended into sleep.

I shall tell here what I remember of my own dream. Dunstan and Nandia had their similar, and yet unique, experiences. I vividly recall seeing Nandia's blue-green eyes. The scene expanded and I saw her project herself into a bedroom where Pimpant was sleeping. I followed close behind, and came to the realization that we were in our dream bodies, but visiting this realm of time and space. Nandia nodded at me and pointed to an adjacent corner of the bedroom. There stood Dunstan, silently waving a greeting to us.

Pimpant's body was snoring loudly, although the noise did little to disturb his sleep. From the center of his torso rose a blue-gray, translucent cord—his astral cord that rose up through the ceiling. We knew we would find the man, in his dream body, at the far end of the cord.

Nandia pointed up, telepathing her desire to find Pimpant. But Dunstan shook his head, and telepathed his desire to find Pimpant's copper. I explained to

Nandia that by keeping it from Pimpant, we could neutralize his telepathic abilities.

Frustration furrowed her brow as she mentally projected her objections. "We needn't meddle with any of Pimpant's abilities. How many times am I going to have to remind you boys that we cannot pursue our ideals by using means that don't reflect those ideals. You can't be thinking that we could successfully dissuade him from the path he's travelling, after depriving him of his telepathic ability?" Both Dunstan and I nodded, realizing that, once again, she was right.

"How about if we leave Pimpant's copper for now, and see what we can learn by simply trusting the law of value fulfillment?" Nandia suggested. Without a moment's hesitation, Dunstan and I readily agreed.

Once again, she gestured upward, and following Pimpant's astral cord, disappeared through the ceiling. Dunstan and I were not far behind. We found ourselves in a small child's bedroom, several floors above Pimpant's. There, the man was seated, holding a young girl in his lap. Tears were flowing down his face as he turned toward us.

After examining the child's energy field, we could see that she was in the final stages of Saragalla.

"Sir, would you wish for our help with this girl's healing?" Nandia asked.

"But what can be done? The doctors say there is no chance for her." Despair was plainly etched across his face. As I examined his aura, I noticed that he was also carrying the taint of Saragalla.

Nandia gently took one of Pimpant's hands and one of his daughter's into her own. Looking intently into his eyes, she said, "Of course she can heal the disease.

You both can. We wouldn't have journeyed here if healing weren't possible. Have you not heard of the wonderful recoveries being made by hospice patients at St. Paul's?'

"Oh, I've heard the rumors," he replied. "But I assumed it was only a ploy to get us to stop plundering the city. I was convinced that you were trying to deceive us, and make us think that Saragalla wasn't fatal—and so hoping that we would then abandon our escape plans. From the very beginning, our plans were to be gone well before the epidemic hit our families. But, it's too late for that now."

A fresh stream of tears burst from his eyes. For several moments he silently sobbed, as the three of us breathed deeply. Then, after wiping his face on his sleeve, he continued. "I have failed the people I love most in this world. There could be no greater despair than knowing I cannot turn back the hands of time."

"Mr. Pimpant, what is your daughter's name?" Somehow, Nandia's gentleness touched a deep well of sadness within the man. With bowed head, a renewed flood of tears interrupted his response. Sobbing aloud, his shoulders heaved as he released a wellspring of grief.

"Dahlia," he finally sighed. Overwhelming loss cast its shadow across his face. "It seems she's nearly dead already ..." Again his shoulders heaved, some inner dam of resistance crumbled, and another cascade of deep sobbing burst forth.

Despite her abduction, Nandia radiated an inspiring warmheartedness toward this man. It left me wondering about my own choice to see Pimpant as an enemy. I decided to change my point of view. After a moment's reflection, I realized that I could look at him as a desperate man, fighting mightily to overcome an inner battle with fear. Suddenly, I felt more at peace. I knew we shared a common dream for the safety and security for ourselves and our loved ones.

Throughout her father's sorrow, Dahlia had been quite lethargic. Now, however, she began to stir as Nandia held her hand.

"Hello Dahlia. My name is Nandia. I know that you're sick. Would you like us to help you get better?"

"Not now, please," the girl muttered. Like her father, she was also struggling, as if trying to find some inner well of strength with which to fight some unseen demon. Finally, she willed herself to talk. "There's something I've been wanting to ask Daddy, but I've been afraid to." Her voice was faint, but a renewed vitality was beginning to sharpen the colors in her energy field.

"It's safe to ask your father anything, Sweetie," Nandia said. "He very much wants to help you." Her voice was softly soothing.

Pimpant quickly interjected. "Of course, Darling," he said. His resonant voice was soft and gentle. "You can ask me anything, anything at all. I promise I will answer you honestly." As soon as he heard his daughter speak, his despair began transforming into hope. Obviously, he would grasp at any chance that she might live.

Dahlia took a deep breath of resolve and then asked, "Daddy, when are you going to stop hurting people?"

Startled, the jeweler glanced up at us. He was obviously shocked that his daughter even knew of his dishonorable actions.

After a moment of stunned reflection, his face then softened. He looked down at Dahlia and intently asserted, "Right now, Sweetheart, right now. I am going to stop right now." Tears of shame again streamed down his face. Wiping his cheeks with the back of his hand, he said, "I thought I was making it safe for our family and for our friends to escape this sickness." He stopped for a long moment to consider his words. "Dahlia, you've helped me see that I was wrong. I have hurt people. But never again. I'm glad you spoke up, my Darling. I'm so very sorry …" His words trailed off, his tears resumed.

"No, Daddy, I thank you!" the girl suddenly came alive. "Thank you very much. Now, I'm much happier. Now, I know I can get better."

As we listened to this courageous child's conversation with her father, the three of us were also in tears.

Wiping her own cheeks, Nandia asked, "Dahlia, would you mind if I give you some healing energy?"

"Yum," she dreamily replied. "Yes, please."

Nandia directed a flow of emerald-green light from her hand into Dahlia's. "Your body will use this energy to heal the sickness," she explained. "Let's start by breathing deeply. Then, I want you to imagine a group of red ants wherever you feel unwell in your body. Can you do that?"

Dahlia closed her eyes and breathed. After her second exhalation, she exclaimed, "Oh, yes, I see them now!" As she focused her mind in this way, areas of her aura began glowing with a reddish tint. Dunstan and I began breathing in concert with the child. Nodding, Nandia offered further instruction.

"Now, imagine the energy that's coming into your

hand as a beautiful green color, and then see that color touching every red ant and turning it into a playful, bright-green ant."

As we watched, the red-tinted areas of Dahlia's aura transformed into a vibrant green hue, slowly at first, then accelerating as she became more confident.

As Dahlia's eyes fluttered open, Dunstan bent toward her and said, "Aye, Bairn, you're strong as an ox, so ya are. But, you'll be wantin' ta rest for this day, child. Will you bring your da to our concert at St. Paul's tomorrow night? There we'll work on some more healin'."

She yawned and softly said, "OK, but you sure talk funny." She began to fall asleep in Pimpant's lap, a smile lighting up her face. Gently, she drifted away—and so did my dream.

Fuzzy images filled the rest of my dreaming that night. I do recall floating with Dunstan and Nandia above a grove of trees. We were playfully chasing each other when I heard Dunstan say, "Ya know, floatin' within the auras of trees revitalizes our own energies." That idea was new to me. Playing with it left me feeling youthful and exuberant.

And, as I awakened, it was that feeling that chaperoned in the daylight that was breaking into my bedroom.

XIII

As the concert day dawned, St. Paul's was alive with activity. Nuns were preparing copper-rich foods in the kitchen. Unkempt gang members were being curried by sisters showering attention that would have flattered a French poodle.

Early that morning, I taught Sister Mary-Agnes pendulum dowsing. With her strong intuitive sense, she was a natural. She wanted to test others and pestered me to show her how to create new remedies. A quick study, her nimble intellect melded well with her intuition. I encouraged her to practice often so she could soon be teaching others.

Working together like a well-oiled machine, a team of nuns continued at the radionics instrument, producing case after case of bottled remedies. Off-duty officers from Krepkie's detail helped Dunstan rehearse the choir. Singers were organized into harmony groups and guided through their entry and exit cues. Father Raphael seemed to be everywhere at once, attending to the thousand-and-one logistical details that the performance demanded. Throughout the day, police vans delivered homeless gangs to the hospice to pick up more remedies and restock themselves with flyers. Then, they set out for new, untouched sections of the city.

It was late morning before Nandia tuned into us telepathically. "No need to worry any longer, boys," she said. "Pimpant has had a complete change of heart, thanks in no small part to your help during last night's dreaming. Right now, we're working with his partners in crime, and helping them give up their avaricious ways. Dahlia is recovering nicely and looking forward to arriving with family and friends. I'll stay with them for the day. Make sure to plan on a big crowd!"

I checked in with her throughout the day, informing her of the rising tide of events that ebbed and flowed through St. Paul's. This was to be my first appearance as an emcee and, like a nervous prima donna, I practiced and changed, and then revised and repracticed my introduction for Angelsong. At one point, Nandia suggested that I instruct the audience both on musical toning and administering the Saragalla remedy. That added a new layer of self-conscious worry. She later informed me that Pimpant, even though exhausted from the effects of Saragalla, wanted to speak from the stage. I liked the sound of that and practiced an introduction for him, as well.

Saint Paul's began filling up a full half-hour before the show was to begin. A crew of ushers, made up of well-groomed gang members sporting distinctive green armbands, hurried into position. Early arrivals, comfortably dressed for a warm summer's evening, were ushered to seats as they chatted nervously, uncertain of what to expect. The evening's soft breezes blessed the cathedral with the sweet scent of jasmine.

At the hospice, Father Raphael had shunted aside empty beds to make room for a final rehearsal. Dunstan was rounding up teens. The Scotsman then ran the choir through their warm-up exercises—breathing to release tensions and singing scales in harmony. Finally, they briefly rehearsed their repertoire of songs.

Father Raphael and Sister Mary-Agnes vacillated between feeling nervous and feeling relieved over the announcement of their wedding. They bustled about, handling countless last-minute details. At one point, they were hurrying around the same corner, each coming from the opposite direction. Preoccupied with their lists of duties, they collided, and fell into each other's arms. Most of us watching did a lousy job of trying to hide our laughter. Looking up, the pair began laughing with us, paused to briefly kiss each other, waved and then hurried on their way.

All three of Geasa's vid stations had crews setting up equipment. I navigated through their cameras and cables looking for Dunstan. I couldn't remember, but it might have been the second time I asked him if he was planning to solo the show's opening. I also asked that he play several of my favorite street tunes.

"Aye, d'na fasch yourself, Laddie "he said, aware of my anxiety. "Your only worry will be what to say to the mobs a' people wantin' to thank you for the grand job you've done."

For some reason, I did not find much comfort in those words. I continued to remind myself of the importance of deep breathing.

Ten minutes before the opening, the wave of people

flowing into St. Paul's showed little sign of abating. As the pews in the nave filled, gang members solemnly ushered people to the last of the standing room along the outer walls. Candle-shaped lights lit up sparkling chandeliers, as their multi-colored reflections bounced off the cathedral's high, ornate ceiling. The church nave was now abuzz with voices of excitement.

Twice, I mentally tapped into Dunstan to ask about his arrival. He ignored my first request. To my second, his response was simply, "Trust, Laddie, trust."

I headed for the front of the church to see if I could help find room for the last of the waiting crowd. On the way, a gentle prod touched my shoulder and I turned to see The Abbot surrounded by a group of monks. That was followed by a second prod from behind, and there was Captain Krepkie with a number of his officers. I warmly greeted both groups and introduced them to each other. I took the opportunity to recount how the monks of St. Martin's had been so vital to our cause.

I was about to sing Captain Krepkie's praises to the monks, when Dunstan's horn rang out. From somewhere high above us, a three-note trill resonated throughout the cavernous space. Its echo was followed by a long, extended, bell-like tone that seemed to last an age before leaning into a delicious fade.

Trust a Scotsman to start early, I thought. Although, I had to admit, his music was calming to the noisy crowd. He next began performing a bluesy solo. By that tune's second bridge, no one was speaking. Aura colors among the audience began intensifying. As I expected, Dunstan's music helped people relax and open their hearts.

A spotlight scanned the stage and nearby walls, frantically searching for the music's source. It finally found the fiery Scotsman playing high above the crowd in a lofty alcove above the church entry. Its former tenant had been a statue of St. Mary. I had to chuckle as I wondered what the musician had done with the now homeless icon.

Dunstan played and jived, keeping tempo with his whole body. People craned their necks to watch the musician from his elevated perch. His eyes rounded at times, as if surprised to be hearing such tones from his horn. At other times, he raised playful, prayerful eyes to the heavens, bending notes that bounced off the cathedral ceiling. The music skipped into a jazz tempo and the crowd below began clapping to the syncopated rhythm.

I resolved to later ask Dunstan for a tour of his past lives, wanting to hear how he had developed such talent. He certainly had this concert's debut well in hand. After watching this masterful performance, I couldn't imagine why I had been worried.

With a flourish, Dunstan added more color to his jazzy number, building a new tempo in a new key. I joined in the sudden eruption of applause as I headed for the stage, navigating through the stranding-room-only crowd that lined the outside aisle. Suddenly, the music shifted location. All I could see in Mary's now-deserted alcove was a faint shimmering of Dunstan's fading aura.

Without missing a beat, the jazzy melody unexpectedly burst from center stage. There, his aura began to reappear, and the musician slowly materialized into his brightly garbed body. His coat and kilt swayed to the beat of his rhythmic dance. Even though his horn was the last thing to appear, the music continued to build. Its volume rose to forte before hitting a crescendo. Dunstan then wove his bridging theme into a soft repeating pattern that melted into a silence and left us all hungry for more.

The standing ovation was spontaneous. Dunstan let the crowd's applause wind down before he bowed and then beckoned his choir on stage. A steady stream of gang members, all who had been rendered homeless by the Saragalla epidemic, flowed in from both sides of the altar. Once assured that their entrance was proceeding apace, the Scotsman began his next tune, a soft jazz, brightly tempoed Tuxedo Junction knock-off. It lasted a full five minutes, covering the time needed for the last of over two hundred youths to settle into tiers.

They jostled each other nervously until Dunstan turned to them and raised his arms, using his horn like a conductor's wand. The choir and audience turned silent, eyes glued to the minstrel, who paused for a moment, and then dropped his arms. With precise timing, the choir began to sing the folk song I so loved:

If the people lived their lives,
as if it were a song for singing out of light,
provides the music for the stars
to be dancing circles in the night.

The choir added harmonies during the song's second repetition. After that, they began singing it in rounds. Brief, but dramatic, horn riffs punctuated three-part harmonies. About the time the choir was reaching the tune's finale, a disturbance near the church entry caused heads to turn.

The cluster of latecomers gathered there made it difficult to tell what was happening. People gradually shuffled aside to reveal Nandia, who was easing her way through the crowd while pushing a wheelchair carrying Pimpant. A radiant Dahlia sat in his lap, looking vibrant and alive. She smiled brightly to all who greeted the trio.

A pathway opened along the nave's outside wall as the three slowly made their way toward the stage. Behind them, a group of Pimpant's followers extended the procession.

I sent a mental image of Pimpant's arrival to Dunstan. He nodded and signaled the choir to repeat its final verse. At the stage steps, Nandia picked up Dahlia. Then, several ushers steadied Pimpant as he stood and mounted the steps, balanced on a pair of crutches. Dunstan brought the singing to a sotto finale, and stepping aside, graciously gestured for me to take over.

After the second round of applause faded, I stepped forward. "Welcome, city of Geasa, to our concert. Tonight, we celebrate the beginning of the end of the Saragalla epidemic," I announced loudly.

That triggered another long round of applause. I nodded to Pimpant and gestured for him to join me at the microphone. As the crowd's noise wound down, I thanked him and said, "I'm very touched that you are with us this evening, Monsieur Pimpant." Holding out my hand, I welcomed him center stage.

He shook my hand, nodded and then handed me his crutches. Despite looking old, pale and tired, a golden-hued energy was streaming through his aura. Waving away an offered stool, he paused, looked out across the audience and then stepped up to the microphone. He cleared his throat, turned to me and flashed a brief smile of gratitude. Then, turning back to the crowd, he spoke: "Thank you for welcoming me, Bernard. I wish to express my deep felt gratitude to you and your companions. Due to your tireless efforts and excellent healing skills, our city has turned back the fatal tide of Saragalla."

Together, the choir and the audience erupted in yet another loud wave of applause. Pimpant waited patiently until it had faded.

"Good people of Geasa, I must speak to you," he began, and paused again. "I wish to apologize to you for the harm I have brought to this community." He then silently looked out over the audience, letting people meet his gaze before continuing.

"I have long believed that most people are against me, that they want to take what is mine. I have interpreted many of your actions in this way. I've recently learned that such distorted thoughts give birth to my own fears—fears which have multiplied through time. In an attempt to ease my fears for my family's safety, I have been walking a path of greed."

His eyes then sought out Nandia. He gestured for her to join him. Taking her hand, he held it high. "This is Nandia. With her help, I have come to understand that I've been pursuing my desires for financial security at the expense of my emotional well-being. He lowered her hand and continued, "I have been terrified of financial ruin and the greater loss of my family. Such imaginings have only served to fuel the growth of more fear. I began making decisions that cost me my self-respect."

He signaled offstage to Dahlia. Noting the gesture, Dunstan gently took the child's hand and escorted her center stage. Pimpant took her into his arms, warmly kissed her cheek and looked out over the crowd. "This is Dahlia, my daughter, whom I love more than life. Only through her loving help, have I finally come to realize how intolerable are my burdens of guilt and shame. I must change."

He handed his daughter back to Dunstan. They proceeded offstage as Pimpant again reached out and took Nandia's hand. "This remarkable woman is quite an effective healer. She has helped me heal my fear and heal my shame. I no longer wish to hide these problems from myself, nor do I wish to continue to hide them from you. That is over."

A hush fell over the church at this proclamation. Pimpant took a deep breath before continuing, "I have conspired with like-minded people, many of whom are corporate and governmental leaders within this city, to rob you of your wealth. Our plan was to leave Geasa for secure homes elsewhere, well in advance of the final, horrible conclusion to the Saragalla epidemic."

"I have learned ..." he paused as he smiled toward Nandia," ... I have learned that explaining myself is not the same as accepting responsibility for my actions. Toward that end, I now assure you that I and my family will remain in Geasa. We will use whatever resources are necessary to restore and rebuild this community.

"We all owe a special note of gratitude to Nandia, Bernard and the wonderful musician, Dunstan. Each of them has traveled from afar to come to our aid. It is through their vast knowledge of healing, and a loving desire to share that knowledge, that we are recovering our health and regaining our self-respect. A special note of thanks is also due to the group of our homeless youths who discovered and shared the very valuable medicinal herb they've named Angelsong. It is only through the open-heartedness of these two groups that I can thankfully say, my daughter has stepped back from death's door and is alive and well today. I also have begun my recovery from Saragalla."

Pimpant lowered his head as a flow of tears cascaded down his cheeks. He grew silent for a moment and then looked up, sharing his sadness with the audience. His sobbing was the only sound penetrating the silence. It was a long, solemn moment before the man gravely lowered his head again. Many heads were bowed throughout the crowd. More than a few faces were awash with tears. It was a profound expression of respect for Pimpant's painful moment of self-revelation.

From the front row of the choir, Sarah stepped forward. She stood next to Pimpant and gently took his hand. "Sir," she somberly said, "please sing a note with me."

She began toning the note she had discovered at our first meeting. Her voice grew in power, and soon choir members, trained in toning, were adding their own individual voices. Their harmony rang richer as more and more singers joined in. Tenuously, Pimpant voiced a baritone note and let the sound build as he gained confidence. Within moments, a glorious harmony rose throughout the church, spilling out into the streets.

The dramatic sound slowly began to abate only

after Pimpant lifted his arms and spread them wide, as if embracing the entire audience. Joy washed across his tear-stained features. He looked out over the crowd for a long, silent moment, and then announced, "You and I shall travel together on this road to recovery. My family thanks you. We will repay our debt to you. I would like to help anyone who shares my fear of poverty. Come and see me, anytime. We'll walk through my garden—your garden now—as we learn to heal together. Father Raphael and Sister Mary-Agnes, you have my complete and unquestioning support for the new direction you are bringing to this church. Use me, for I can be of help working with the hierarchy."

He wobbled a bit, turned and slowly settled into the wheelchair being steadied by Nandia. They both humbly bowed to the thunderous applause of the audience. After a final wave together, she wheeled Pimpant offstage. Dozens of eager hands helped lower him to the floor.

As three street-dressed gang members began clearing the way for Pimpant's departure, the sound of Dunstan's horn again pierced the air. He trilled three electrifying notes, the same dynamic riff that had earlier galvanized the crowd. Instantly on its feet, the audience applauded throughout Pimpant's departure.

Center stage, Dunstan introduced a new, dramatic duet, a jazzy calypso tune, that was sung in beautiful syncopated rhythms by the choir. As the youngsters accompanied their words by clapping in tempo, the audience joined in, as well.

At this point, I directed the youths who were carrying remedy bottles to spread out along the outside aisles of the church. They all knew that I would soon be calling upon them to hand out the remedy.

As Dunstan's duet wound down, I mounted the stage again and introduced Angelsong. "I'm very happy to announce that the discovery of this herb was first made by a band of homeless youths, one of whom learned of its power in a dream. We would never have found these young people, nor Angelsong, were it not for the invaluable aid of The Abbot and monks of St. Martin's monastery. To them, we owe a huge debt of gratitude. With their help, we have created a vibrational form of this herb for anyone who would like to try it. Simply raise your hands and bottles of the remedy will be passed to you."

While the bottles were being handed out, I explained the safety and dosages of vibrational remedies. I then invited Nandia and Sarah to join me at the microphone. I knew that, together, they would—more gracefully than I ever could—guide people to combine musical toning with their first dose of the remedy. As soon as Nandia had given instructions, Sarah began toning. People took the allotted doses and then began testing their voices, seeking to find their own notes. The earlier toning session with Pimpant allowed many in the audience to do this quite comfortably.

I watched people's energy fields and was amazed at how quickly muddy-brown colors transformed into green, blue and gold hues. The vibrancy of their auras was being restored! A natural harmony grew from the collective toning that reverberated throughout the nave. Dunstan complemented the sound with a combination of three-note riffs on his horn.

The healing effect was mesmerizing. People stood,

with radiant smiles of great joy on their faces. It took a while before the toning came to its natural close. Then, there was quite an extended applause for Nandia and Sarah, who held hands and bowed repeatedly before departing the stage. Stepping over to the microphone, I explained that the Angelsong remedy, as well as St. Martin's herbal tinctures, were available at St. Paul's hospice.

I then announced, "Father Raphael has been working on a very exciting new direction for this church. I would like to invite him to the stage to share his story and his plans with you."

The priest calmly stepped up to the microphone. "Many of us, myself included, have feared this Saragalla epidemic," he began. "I have since learned that my fears are born out of my beliefs in contagion. These are sadly mistaken beliefs, I assure you! I am not powerless in the face of illness. None of us are! I have learned that whenever I use my powerful consciousness to blame others for my illnesses, my fears spread like wildfire, threatening to turn to ashes all that is sacred in my life.

"We have blamed truant school children for being the originators of this disease. Our church has added to that illusion by teaching that a wrathful God delivered Saragalla to punish the guilty. We have encouraged the sick to believe that Saragalla cannot be healed, that their suffering will only get worse. I am very sorry to say that we of the clergy have taught the mistaken belief that only through suffering can we recover our worth, our holiness and God's love.

"Nandia has helped me accept the truth of my power as an individual. I am learning to accept the power of my beliefs, and to trust my innate power to heal.

"Nandia has helped me learn that the real reason for suffering is to learn that there is absolutely no need for suffering. Blaming others for our misfortunes is to deny that each of us is the creator of our own misfortunes. Nandia has helped me accept that I alone am creating my life, that I alone am responsible for my well-being. To accept this power means to accept that my thoughts ultimately shape my reality. We do live in God's loving universe, not one that seeks to punish us. Every part of life is of loving intent! The mistaken belief that pathogens seek to destroy us greatly compromises our innate ability to heal."

By now, Raphael's pitch had grown to a riveting intensity. His delivery and his energy captured people's attention. "By blaming children for this epidemic, we have refused to accept that each of us has the natural power to hold ourselves above violation and harm. Believing that truant children spread this disease, we have polarized our community. Families have disintegrated.

"Beliefs in humankind's imperfection, unworthiness and unreliability create illness by encouraging us to accept guilt and punishment. I know now that suffering, punishment and pain will never rescue us from the degraded states we create for ourselves. In truth, we are each individual beings of good intent. We are here to learn of our own power to transform energy. We create every part of our individual experience. No being but the individual has such power. This is the new direction toward which I wish to guide this church."

In that moment, you could have heard a pin drop. In the next, thunderous applause. The priest stood quietly, looking out over the audience. He then asked Sister Mary-Agnes to join him. They clasped hands and the priest continued, "This is Sister Mary-Agnes. I love this woman. I am ashamed to say that I have been hiding my love for her, fearful of its consequences. It was Nandia who showed me that expressing my feelings honestly is the necessary first step toward respecting myself—the unique expression of God that I am.

"My beloved and I will soon be announcing our wedding date. It is our wish that our betrothal will be a catalyst to bring about loving change to this church."

As Father Raphael spoke, I watched the auras of several cassock-clad priests sitting among the audience. Their energy fields were filled with the lovely deep blue and violet colors of wonder and excitement. It seemed to me that he was already generating support from among the clergy of St. Paul's.

"No matter what the consequences of our love, Sister Mary-Agnes and I will continue to serve those in this community who seek spiritual support," he continued. "I ask you all to join us here on Sunday. Together, we will begin to change our beliefs in a wrathful god. We will begin to replace the doctrine of original sin with the notion of original innocence."

A round of generous applause showered the two beaming clerics. They hugged each other and bowed together, several times. As they were leaving the stage, Dunstan again hefted his horn like a baton. With a broad smile and a decided flourish, he dropped his arms, so beginning the choir's closing song.

This last number had been delightfully choreographed. Smiles erupted throughout the audience as we watched gang members mirroring Dunstan's characteristic jives while he accompanied their singing. Some among the audience stood and danced as well, all the while adding their own voices to fill the cathedral.

As the applause for a second encore began to fade, I mounted the steps to the stage for the last time, inviting Nandia and Dunstan to stand with me. I took their hands as I spoke. "In searching for answers for Saragalla, I have been thrice blessed. I have met these two exceptional individuals, and I have grown in their presence. I have also learned that much of my life's limitation has been the result of blaming the church of my childhood for my choices to see myself as guilty, tainted and needing punishment. Through helping people heal this disease, I have learned that no choice has ever been thrust upon me. I only accepted ideas of diminishment and limitation because they fit my distorted ideas about myself at the time.

"I have been inspired by the people of Geasa and by your desire to accept your own power to heal. Being with you as you have healed has helped me to heal. I am deeply grateful. I thank you."

I then nodded to Nandia, who simply added, "My heartfelt thanks go out to all of you. To have had the chance to serve you has been a gift and a privilege I will never forget. I love you."

Smiling broadly, Dunstan nodded in agreement. He pointed to the choir and called out, "And these wanderin' vagabonds have shown us that they can sing!"

With that, the crowd went wild. Wolf whistles, cat calls and deafening applause echoed throughout the church. Choir members forced embarrassed smiles, found interesting details in their shoes, and plucked lint from each other's clothes.

As the raucous noise wound down, Dunstan added, "Many thanks to Police Captain Krepkie and his fine men for showin' us that, workin' together, we can repair torn families. As Geasa continues to recover, some of you may wish to add youngsters to your homes," He gestured toward the choir as he continued. "If so, before you go home this evening, come meet these rascals out front of the church. If you find one you would like to know better, let them take you for a wander through the city. Or, you may decide you'd like to invite them to dinner. They each know how to eat, of that I'm certain. If you meet any you're not sure of, bring 'em to me and I'll string 'em up by their thumbs 'til their haloes shine." After widespread laughter, there followed enthusiastic applause for the charismatic Scotsman.

He flashed the choir his infectiously loving grin and picked up his horn.

The evening ended with a final solo, during which Dunstan disappeared and reprised his position once again, perched high above the entry in St. Mary's alcove.

The clamorous applause echoed throughout the nave for quite a while before people reluctantly began filing out of the church. Then, from his lofty perch, Dunstan resumed his delightful music until the last of the audience had departed. At that point, all of the choir members and dozens of ushers from homeless gangs began wildly cheering. Their faces were more brightly radiant than any saint's could ever have been.

XIV

OVER BREAKFAST THE NEXT MORNING, Nandia, Dunstan and I talked of our mixed feelings over this, our final day. I shared my characteristic dread at the prospect of a long string of farewells that was sure to dog our steps. "I just don't like goodbyes," I complained. "They remind me too much of loss. But, I suppose goodbye is preferable to disappearing without a word."

We breathed together as we acknowledged the loss we each were experiencing. Of course, Dunstan mentioned his choirs, Nandia recapped warm moments spent with Father Raphael and Sister Mary-Agnes, and I recalled how inspired I was by the young man who had recovered from the terminal ward. We reminisced over our experiences with The Abbot, Krepkie, Sarah, Pimpant and Dahlia as we made our way to the hospice. Then Nandia the Wise reminded us that we might even enjoy discovering how the city of Geasa was handling the concert's aftermath.

It didn't take long to find out. Arriving at the

hospice, we were met by a long line of Geasans waiting to pick up remedies. Having heard favorable stories from concert-goers and the news media, their line spilled out the front door and beyond St. Paul's courtyard.

Inside, nuns were in full swing at the radionics instrument. Apparently, demand for the Saragalla remedy was on the rise. "Aye, yur as steady as clockwork, so y'are," Dunstan crowed. "Just watchin' you lovelies at work makes me want to lay down and rest." I caught several of the women blushing—I suspect they were embarrassed to have captured the notice of a man such as the Scotsman. We wandered through the wards, where we found patients and staff calmly waiting in line to hug us and shake our hands.

Captain Krepkie stopped by just before midday to let us know that hospitals around the city were releasing patients and paring down their waiting lists. He also announced that the governor had lifted the proscription against owning copper.

"He's promised to return Geasa's copper to her treasury!" he exclaimed. This brought shouts of delight from those listening and intensified hopes for the city's economic recovery.

Krepkie then took me aside and said, "By the way, all the charges against the three of you have been dropped. But, if he wants to continue playing music, the Scotsman will have to get a busker's license." We had a good laugh over that. As we parted, he wished us safe travels.

People were abuzz over the news that confiscated copper would be returned to its rightful owners. A news report stated that the treasury had begun minting new copper five-rhyal coins, ten of which were to be distributed to every adult throughout the city. Banks were responding by offering no-interest loans to help businesses and families rebuild.

Among those present, optimism soared. People delighted in sharing their wish lists for greater prosperity. There was talk of planning family holidays, to near and far Fantibo. Dreams were shared with expectations of delight, from new homes to new shoes. Amidst this revelry, Father Raphael and Sister Mary-Agnes stopped by to invite us to their wedding.

"Sorry, but we can't be here for your grand day," Nandia apologized. "We've only a narrow window of time in which to return home. But, if the energies should change before the wedding, I'll be back, with bells on, bearing sparkly gifts and love. I can think of several outfits, Sister, that will flatter you and get you out of that bad habit." We groaned in unison as Sister Mary-Agnes laughed graciously at that over-used pun.

A bit later on, The Abbot and St. Martin's contingent of monks dropped by to say farewell. He thanked me for the case of vibrational remedies and asked if he could send several monks to the convent to learn how to dowse and use the radionics equipment. Sister Mary-Agnes enthusiastically agreed to be their teacher.

"We will probably have to wait until the next crisis to identify the malcontents at the monastery," The Abbot added. "They've gone underground since you so effectively diffused my brother and his group."

He looked bemused as he watched me work to untangle that riddle. Then it hit me why I had noticed that familiar cast to his eyes the day we met. The

Abbot was Pimpant's brother! As I looked into his eyes once again, he telepathed the thought: "Although my brother and I have been distant since childhood, we've watched each other's lives unfold with the greatest interest. And, now, I'm to be my cousin's best man!" As I listened in amazement, I came to see how three men, related by blood, each uniquely expressed the wellspring of strength that flowed through their common bloodline.

Dunstan announced that he was staying on in Geasa. "Aye, I've been here too long to want t' go home now. What's another year or two, when there's so much music to be made? And, I'm thinkin', that with the copper-rich diet ya found, there'll be a number of these young varmints wantin' to use their telepathic and teleportation abilities. Seems to me what Geasa needs now is a good teacher. So, any time the two of ya are ready ta get into some real work, I could use your help."

We were all in tears as he hugged us both.

After the soon-to-be-newlyweds departed, Nandia grabbed my hand and took me aside. She soberly told me she would be returning to her family, a husband and a daughter. "As a matter of fact, I've three other families, some with great-grandchildren long since departed."

The news kicked me in the pit of my stomach. I was too upset to ask about her age. I had to admit that I had felt a nagging disquiet about pursuing a romance, but had shuffled those doubts to the back of my mind. And still, I grieved the loss of the dreams I had of being with this beautiful and most intriguing woman.

Nandia reminded me that my thoughts and

feelings were playthings with which to make growing fun. "That, of course, never ends," she said. Then she laughed and kissed me. But I was pouting too much to accept comfort from her.

I knew that my pain was a messenger telling me of some distortion about how I viewed the situation, but all I wanted to do at the moment was pity myself and blame both of us. At that point, she said, "I do know you love me. And you'll love me regardless of this missed opportunity for romance."

Silently, I withdrew.

I isolated myself at the end of the pew where Nandia and I had first met Father Raphael. I repeatedly cast aside the intruding memory of our talk about value fulfillment that we'd begun on this very spot. Instead, I stewed and sulked, certain that my dreams for greater intimacy were lost forever.

After a time, Dunstan came over and sat next to me. "I ken y'er sufferin' Lad, but ya've lost sight of why. The only true reason any of us creates sufferin' is to finally learn there's not a reason in this grand world of ours for sufferin'.

"So, when you're done blamin' yourself and punishin' people, Laddie, remember that punishment is always about a loss of self-respect. And, I'll make bail that ya must be believin' that this loss is nae an expression of value fulfillment. Ya must be believin' that your exalted dreams somehow justify using these means. But, the plain fact is that punishment is like barbed wire to growth. Ya'll not now, nor will you ever, recover your self-respect through punishin' yourself or Nandia like this."

To Dunstan, I was willing to listen. I knew he was

right. I began a series of connected breaths and, unexpectedly, a torrent of tears followed. I let go and let myself cry out my sadness.

As my sobs subsided, I looked up through blurred eyes and thanked the Scotsman. "I did, after all, let myself love Nandia regardless of the possibility of loss," I admitted. As the giant musician hugged me, I felt myself a boy again, being held by my father.

I sought out Nandia and embraced her as I apologized. We talked of looking forward to being together in front of the Grand Council. She saw that I was still hurting over my loss, and asked, "Bearns, would you mind if I kissed you?"

My first reaction was again one of a little boy pouting. As I felt myself closing down again, I was tempted to lash out with, "I'm never going to let you love me again." But this, I knew, was more of my need to punish. I quickly asked the energy within that hurt to transform itself into my trusting the truth of just how much I am loved. At that point, it was easy to see just how much I did want that kiss.

We put our backs into it, as if answering a dream. Parting, she placed her lips next to my ear, and softly sang, "The universe does love you. That includes me, it's true, 'tis true. We've always loved you, and always will." I looked into her beautiful eyes and could see how true that was.

I was at peace.

We made our way to the hospice, where many young folk, nuns, and recovering patients had gathered to say their final farewells. I looked out over a sea of faces, shining with gratitude, all waiting to express their love and affection.

Wanting to speak from my heart, I took a breath and said, "I'm speechless. But, as usual, not for very long. Meanwhile, could we breathe together?"

People chuckled as we fell silent, breathing deeply. I inhaled fully and looked into the eyes of so many men and women I had been given the chance to love. I began toning a deep, resonant note, and soon everyone in the crowd had joined in with their own individual tones. Tears welled up and tumbled down faces as the sound grew. Dunstan picked up his horn and played a mournful tune that melted into a joyful lullaby. We gathered together, expressing both our loss and our gratitude to each other.

After more deep breathing, I said, "I have never before had the privilege of supporting a cause as magnificent as Geasa's recovery to health. I have received many gifts from your love. I have learned from you and grown with you. I thank you. I thank you. And you know of my penchant for repeating myself. I return home today, and will carry you all in my heart. My great hope is that somewhere in time, we will be together again."

With eyes radiant with love, Nandia rose up into the air and began singing,

"If the people lived their lives,
as if it were a song for singing out of light ..."

... and her energy field began to shimmer and fade. As the familiar spiral of white light filled my head, I felt one last invisible kiss and, once again, Nandia disappeared.

Preview of Book II of The Nandia Trilogy

NANDIA'S APPARITION

HAVING JUST TELEPORTED from the dank and gloomy chambers of the Galactic Grand Council, we suddenly appeared in the middle of a gaily decorated ballroom. It was packed shoulder-to-shoulder with waltzing couples. The mixture of perfumery from both genders, as malodorous as varnish remover, was in stark contrast to the musky atmosphere from which we had just departed.

Feeling the warmth of Nandia's hands nestled in mine, I began slowly swaying to the music. Thankfully she followed, apparently familiar with this shuffle-and-glide two-step number that had been arranged to fit a waltz tempo.

Then, I stopped. I released her hands, bowed and innocently asked, "Has this dance been taken?" With her usual angelic smile, Nandia settled into my arms and off we sailed. Neither of us wanted to be the only motionless couple in this undulating sea of dancers. It was bad enough that we were the only ones not

wearing the ornately gilt-edged garb that was currently in favor at King Sabre's court.

The monarch was seated, slightly askew, on a throne
at the far end of the dance floor. Occasionally, he drib-
bled wine from the glass he so casually held. A gaggle
of supplicants minded him, all as anxious to please as
the highest paid geishas back home on Earth.

Guards were stationed along the ballroom's outer
walls. Their over-embellished uniforms competed
with sparkly chandeliers that were trimmed in colorful floral garlands. A formally attired orchestra played
planet Aesir's latest music.

Yet, despite the court's well-appointed opulence,
most people looked troubled. Their auras were muddy,
their voices low, their sentences clipped. I asked
Nandia if she thought they seemed preoccupied, as if
disturbed by a nagging guilt over some secret crime.
Peering over my shoulder, she scanned the ballroom.
We were well in step with the flow of dancers that
circulated the dance floor. And, we were gliding ever
closer to the King. I stooped a bit to better blend in.

"From what I'm picking up," Nandia telepathed,
resting her head once again upon my cheek, "many are
here in the hopes of finding some thread of redemp-
tion for the woes of the kingdom. And, no one is being
reassured by the antics of the King or his minions."

One of the reasons we had been selected by the
Grand Council for this mission was the effectiveness
of our telepathic communication. I was glad that, here
on Aesir, I could so easily hear her thoughts.

It is often said that everyone has telepathic abilities. However, many of us won't use them for fear of

exposing our true thoughts and feelings. We mostly send messages through our energy fields that say, "Don't get too close, I'm hiding." Hypocrisy cannot be telepathed.

When we first met at the Grand Council briefing that had launched an earlier adventure on the planet Fantibo, Nandia and I had found that we trusted each other implicitly. Naturally, with such transparent openness, we telepathed quite easily. It had saved our lives more than once on Fantibo, despite the fact that our mental connection there had initially been short-circuited.

I enjoyed the scent of Nandia's hair on my cheek. I also reveled in how she felt in my arms. But, these first moments of our new mission were not the time to indulge such feelings. Instead, I recalled a previous Council delegate's attempts to extricate King Sabre from his tangled affairs on Aesir. Needless to say, he had failed.

Reports were that Sabre still blamed that delegate for the precipitous decline in his planet's economy. And, rather than accept responsibility for his own misdeeds, the King condemned the same delegate for planting the rumors that he was coming unhinged. Upon hearing that bit of news, the monarch had thrown one of his more noteworthy tantrums. Figuring in the list of Sabre's woes included a palace haunting by the shade of the King's father, plus an unhealthy dependence upon alcohol.

As Council delegates, we had been directed to restore some semblance of order to Aesir's royal house. At the very least, this required that we befriend this garrulous monarch. But, I had not the slightest idea how we might inveigle ourselves into Sabre's good graces.

I did, however, have a pretty good idea that Nandia and I, the latest hope of the Grand Council, would not find ourselves in the King's good graces, should our first meeting occur while two-stepping about on his dance floor.

Nandia reminded me that Aesir's news reports had compared the King's penchant for public outbursts to that of a petulant child. He was notoriously cranky when faced with disappointment. My partner also reminded me that, with every gliding step, we were dancing closer to being discovered. "Bearns," she telepathed with an attention-getting note of alarm, "we need to get out of here, now!"

Spotting an exit down a side hallway, I guided us obliquely through the crowd in that direction. I only rushed the orchestra's tempo ever so slightly to make good our escape. Several couples stopped talking as we glided by. A few brows wrinkled quizzically in reaction to our out-of-fashion, dark attire. Thankfully, only a few eyes stole curious glances to look at our faces. I was relieved that we were being ignored by most.

As we navigated across the dense tide of dancing couples, I wondered what this event was celebrating. Nandia picked up on my question, tilted her head to the left and telepathed, "Behind us, there's a tall blonde who seems interested in you. She just remarked to her partner that this thirtieth anniversary of Sabre's coronation doesn't hold a candle to the celebration of ten years ago."

I glanced over Nandia's shoulder to see if we were

attracting the King's attention. At that moment, he was being distracted by a wine steward. I sailed us out of sight down our getaway hall.

"I didn't know you could dance so well," Nandia said, as we nonchalantly hurried down the corridor seeking further sanctuary from prying eyes.

"Someday, we'll have to find out just how well you can keep up," I bragged. "We wouldn't have escaped the King's notice if that orchestra had been playing a tango."

Nandia grabbed my arm and led me though an archway into a darkened library. As we stepped through the doorway, her arms encircled my neck. She graced my lips with a kiss that took my breath away. Parting, she whispered, "It's lovely to be working with you again, Bearns. Now, do you have any bright ideas as to how we're going to meet this King?

It took a moment for me to catch my breath. As I did, I scanned our surroundings, noting that we were well concealed. "We're probably safe here for the moment," I said. "But, I'm betting that by this evening's end, several of Sabre's meddling minions will have mentioned the off-world couple who appeared from out-of-the-blue and danced off into the night."

Suddenly, I had a mental image of the two of us waiting in Sabre's bedchambers. The scene evolved into a view of the inebriated King returning to his chambers. The two of us respectfully stood, stepped forward with hands outstretched and formally introduced ourselves.

"I've just had an idea," I said. "Although, it seems a little crazy to me."

"Come on, Bearns, spill," Nandia prodded.

"Well, we could find Sabre's bedchambers and be waiting for him when he returns from this celebration." As I said these words, I had to grimace. It was just plain crazy! I would just as soon attempt to ride a donkey down a flight of stairs. We had no idea how to find the royal chambers. We had a very good idea of his state of inebriation. And to top that off, we had no idea what his bedroom looked like.

Teleportation does not work without a mental image to use as a target. If we were to weave our way through this palace maze, whether by teleportation or on foot, we simply needed more information. A map, a guidebook, or, even better, a tour guide would have been nice.

I sincerely hoped that here on Aesir, we could teleport our way out of tight spots. It was another of the reasons we had survived on Fantibo. Not only had we faced telepathic disruptions early in that mission, but we found our teleporting abilities thwarted, as well.

It was only after I'd recalled an ancient water dowser's story that we found the answer to that problem. He told a very useful tale of the day his dowsing had failed—the day he had divined three dry wells. After returning to his lab, he discovered that the metal copper resolved the problem. We used his remedy, plus some skillful maneuvering on Nandia's part, to recover the abilities we were afraid we'd lost.

One lesson that experience had taught us was that we needed to test-drive our teleporting abilities before counting on them. And, all the sooner, all the better.

However, this was not the problem at the moment. I was finding no comfort in anticipating the risks of waiting for a king in his bedchambers. Sabre could arrive with a sleeping partner, which would spawn a whole host of unfortunate complications. I knew that if I were suddenly surprised by two strangers after a drunken entrance into my own bedroom, my explosion would certainly rival any of the King's well-known outbursts.

"Right, then," Nandia interrupted my musing. She has a tendency to eavesdrop telepathically, which was at times annoying, but this time was helpful. "It seems clear that your idea isn't the way to meet the King," she telepathed. "What say, instead, we introduce ourselves to this ghost who has a predilection for haunting his own son?"

To even consider her suggestion honestly, I had to face the feeling of disquiet that I'd been hoping to avoid. It was a feeling I'd had ever since I'd heard of the ghost in King Sabre's court.

Reluctantly, I breathed into a tightness that was lightly clutching the center of my abdomen. I let myself accept that sensation and breathed deeply again. I was surprised to realize that there sat a fear of meeting a ghost. As I touched the feeling and asked for insight, the fear suggested I examine my attitudes for prejudice.

I certainly found one. Disembodied entities are largely unknown to me. As a child, I'd been exposed to my culture's fears of poltergeists, and absorbed a bit of those. Early in my studies, it was true, I'd learned techniques for dispelling such beings. But, I was quite disinclined to meet a discarnate who was deviling his own son. That came under the heading of unusually perverse behavior for any father—living or dead.

At that moment, the image of Agoragon, my mentor, flashed across my mind. He reminded me to trust that we have abundant inner resources to look after our own well-being.

"Bernard, you've again forgotten that you always have the power to hold yourself above violation," he would scold whenever I took on the victim's role, hiding from fear and hoping for sympathy. But, I'd never tested that particular power while dealing with cranky, disembodied royalty.

So, I was frightened to meet this ghost. Yet, I knew that Nandia's plan made a lot more sense than my crazy idea. And, how difficult could it be to find some common ground with a spook? After all, each of us is fundamentally a disembodied spirit, anyway. Despite my occasional mistrust of the idea, I had to remind myself that every being, whether in this dimension or some other, is basically of good intent.

No, I'd say my true apprehensions about a ghostly encounter were due to my occasional inclinations toward rudeness. I could make paint peel off walls if I felt someone was trying too hard to crowd me into a corner. An early teacher had likened me to a bull in a china shop. In those days I tended to impulsively explode over even petty irritations. In time, I learned to calm such storms by using Agoragon's deep-breathing exercises.

He was effusive in his recitations about the value of ten deep, connected breaths. He would preach of the oxygenating and detoxifying benefits until I consciously began deep breathing through my impatience and irritation.

"There are proponents of this discipline who swear

that breathing is all that is needed to heal any disease," he often remarked.

Still, I had no idea how I might react to being cornered by an apparition. I did find reassurance in knowing that only once in a blue moon did my paint-peeling indulgences get the best of me.

And, on the bright side, we just might befriend this spirit, and so learn how to approach his son. It was glaringly obvious that we needed to cultivate allies, regardless of whether or not they occupied a physical body. Luckily, both Nandia and I were equipped with an intuitive sense about whom to trust—yet another advantage that had proven useful on Fantibo.

I had assumed that the reason for our most recent Council summons was to congratulate us for our success on that planet. A little over two years ago, Nandia and I had teleported to Fantibo's city of Geasa. We quickly found an ally in Dunstan—a marooned Council envoy, on-planet for more than a decade. He was a charismatic and flamboyant Scottish musician, whose masterful horn-playing had opened many doors during the mission. He had a unique style of Gaelic humor and a playful flair for the dramatic. Without him, we would have surely failed in our attempts to assist Geasa in its recovery from the Saragalla epidemic.

Yes, the Grand Council had given a quick nod to our work in Geasa, but their true purpose was to brief us about problems on the planet Aesir.

"We must give some credibility to the rumors that Aesir's royal palace is haunted," said the alien Council Elder, whom I had privately named Liberace. It was because of his ornate gowns and outlandish manner that I had bestowed that name upon him. "The King has been complaining of nighttime disturbances by a ghost," he continued. "Many castle residents have corroborated his stories. Sleep deprivation combined with excessive alcohol consumption have added to the monarch's growing anger and hostility. Reports are that his mental and emotional stability is deteriorating. He grants royal commissions to incompetent friends. Corruption and graft are endemic. Aesir's economy is showing signs of unraveling while major corporations are moving many operations off-world. Unemployment is rising, debt growing and inflation nearly out of control. But, that's not all! Recently, there have been rumors of an attempted coup d'état."

He paused to wipe his forehead with a large, embroidered handkerchief. Then his voice dropped to a loud whisper, dripping with distain. "Indeed, one of our previous delegates on Aesir did turn renegade.

"Imagine, a delegate from this very Council! King Sabre's paranoia has led to accusations that we purposefully sent such a man to poison his court. Of course, that is nothing but an absurdity." This last assertion was so loud that it echoed throughout the chamber.

Liberace again wiped his brow, and then cleared his throat. He seemed to be enjoying the drama of his performance. "This Council admired your ingenuity with the Geasa affair. We now have great hopes that you can help Aesir return to some semblance of respectability. You may go now."

With a flamboyant flourish of his bejeweled hands, we were dismissed. A council functionary stepped forward with a stack of Aesir's currency and wished us well. After exchanging quizzical frowns, Nandia and I faced each other and clasped hands—the position used whenever teleporting in tandem. I felt the familiar spiral of white energy expanding through my consciousness and suddenly the drab Chamber of the Grand Council dissolved into King Sabre's ballroom.

As sparse as the whiskers on his head, Liberace's briefing certainly could have been more enlightening. It raised many more questions than it answered. We did know that our first meeting with the King had to build a solid foundation for trust. Otherwise, there was no chance the troubled monarch would rebuild his relationship with the Grand Council.

I had a pretty good idea that Nandia's presence would help do the trick. We had squeaked through several tight spots on Geasa because we men are so powerfully attracted to her.

Leaving those reminiscences behind, Nandia and I carefully re-entered the corridor. We were eager to get started investigating King Sabre's palace and, despite my misgivings about facing a discarnate spirit, Nandia's idea was the best one we had at the moment.

"Let's go meet the King's ghost of a father—if only to find out what he's made of." Only a touch of feigned bravado tainted my words.

"But, before we go," I continued, "we need to find out if we can teleport here on Aesir. Meet me at the far end of the hallway?"

I pointed toward the corridor's end, where hung a portrait of what appeared to be a former Aesirian king. The life-sized painting portrayed a young man, regally seated upon a scarlet throne holding a golden scepter. Dark-haired, fit and handsome, he was attired in an officer's uniform, replete with a glittering array of stripes, pips and medals precisely lined up in several rows across his chest.

Nandia closed her eyes, breathed deeply and disappeared. I watched the golden-red-violet hues of her aura shimmering away before searching for her at the far wall. There, those same vibrating colors began to appear faintly, grew in intensity and finally materialized into her body.

She was smiling as she reached out with wide-opened arms. Then, planting hands on hips, she frowned, tapped her foot and telepathed, "I'm waiting Bearns ... I'm waiting ..."

Breathing deeply, I began my teleportation discipline. I started by imagining the cells of my body being playfully filled with white light, an energy emanating from my Inner Self. I caught a fleeting glimpse of Agoragon, reminding me that energy always follows thought. It was one way he encouraged me to accept the unlimited power of my consciousness. I intensified my focus, seeing my cells overflowing with energy and felt the familiar rush of tingling throughout my body.

I next envisioned a single cell from my heart and projected it to Nandia's location. I knew that my desire combined with my imagination would activate a wave of energy from my body. I directed that wave to follow the seed cell. Then I asked my subconscious to project my body's field of ions, atoms and molecules to follow that wave of energy. Instantly, the familiar spiraling of white light flooded my mind and I quickly found myself standing in front of Nandia. I felt like I was seeing her for the first time—and once again, her beauty startled me.

"That was fun," I said, as we hugged. "Even if we

don't know our way around here, we do know how to get there."

"So, My Dear, do you have any bright ideas of how we're going to meet this ghost?" I asked.

"Meeeouw," came the response.

"Excuse me?" I asked Nandia, wondering why she'd chosen to imitate a cat.

She shook her head, letting me know that the sound hadn't come from her. She turned and pointed down the hallway. I caught a glimpse of a black cat just as it disappeared around a corner. Its feet flashed white as it scampered away.

"That cat just appeared out of nowhere, at exactly the same moment you mentioned the ghost," Nandia explained. "I wonder—it could be telepathic as well! Let's go find out." She raced out of sight around the corner, hot on the critter's trail.

I wasn't far behind as we arrived at a doorway off a second hallway. But the cat was nowhere to be seen. I tried the door and found it locked. The sound of my fumbling was answered by a second "Meeeouw," this time from the other side of the door.

I extracted my lock pick from its pouch and quickly unlocked the door. As it swung open, we saw our four-legged guide ascending a long stairway, bereft of any patience for those with fewer limbs.

Nandia quickly projected herself to the head of the stairs. "Keep moving, Bearns. I'm not going to stand around admiring your burgling skills when we've got ghosts to meet."

I quickly joined her. I decided to follow her instincts about trusting this creature. This was fun, this teleport-tag.

We followed the cat up three flights of stairs before chasing it down another long hallway. Finally, it stopped at an open utility closet. There a chambermaid was loading a cart with towels, monogrammed with Aesir's royal crest.

Slight in stature, the woman was fair-haired and quite pretty. Inexplicably, she carried herself with an ancient, yet youthful, elegance. As she looked up from her work, I was touched by her unusually bright, blue eyes. She then flashed a beautifully dimpled smile that immediately warmed my heart.

However, just as I was about to say hello, she stooped to pet the cat. "Good job, Arcturus." Her words musically chimed with praise. "I was beginning to think you were going to have trouble with these two."

It was a new experience, being led by a small, furry creature. As only cats can, it soaked up the maid's affection, purring with eyes at half-mast. There were spots of white fur highlighting each of its toes. That accounted for the glow we'd seen as he scurried down the dimly lit hallways.

It was heartwarming to watch the mutual displays of affection between the beauty and the beast. The chambermaid then straightened up and graced us with a second winning smile.

"Hello," I said. "This is Nandia. My name is Bernard."

Her eyes radiated a warmth and devotion that spoke of centuries of loving service to Aesir's royal family. Right away, I sensed that I could trust her implicitly.

"We are here at the request of the Grand Council," I explained. "We hope to befriend King Sabre and become useful allies. Our mission is to help unravel the torments that haunt him," I explained.

"Welcome, Bernard and Nandia." The maid curt-seyed with a grace borne of many years of practice. "My name is Elli. I know of your assignment. I had the good fortune to watch your arrival in the ballroom. The two of you dance divinely." As I listened, I realized her lips had not moved. This woman was telepathic as well.

"Thank you Elli," Nandia telepathed in response. "Tonight was our first attempt at dancing. Bearns, as he likes to be called, even challenged me to a tango to test my mettle. Perhaps, if time allows, we might all go dancing together."

That evoked yet another smile. "Now, that's a lovely idea," Ellie agreed.

She bent and picked up Arcturus. "My friend here is telepathically quite articulate. But, being a cat, he can be a bit standoffish until he gets to know you. He wants to know, Bearns, if you're related to King Sabre in any way. He thinks you are the very image of his father of eighty years ago."

I was stunned to think that I looked like a younger version of the castle ghost.

Then it dawned on me why the Council had chosen me for this mission. My outer, rational mind went into overdrive. "This has to be more than just a coincidence! Why didn't someone on the Council tell me?"

With that, I glanced accusingly at Nandia. "Surely, someone must have thought that our resemblance could have some bearing on this mission. Why is it, that once again, I'm the last person to find out about these things?"

Both women chuckled at this. Nandia ignored my semi-serious accusation and went on to explain our plan to Elli.

"We want to assist King Sabre in whatever way we can. We know we follow a failed Council mission that has left a bitter taste in his mouth. His relationship with the Grand Council is a shambles. We were hoping to find Sabre's bedchambers, so we can meet this ghost who is haunting the King."

"I like the plan, Nandia," Elli replied. "And, please, call me El.

"Bearns, if I may say so, you do look like a younger version of King Sabre's father, the old goat," she continued. "Wilhelm is his name, and these days, he resembles you only ever so slightly. But, Nandia, you won't find him in the King's chambers for several more hours. He usually arrives as his son is about to retire. Then, the hell-raising lasts until dawn.

"You should know that we do have a ghost charmer here," she pointed at the cat. "Arcturus has the ghoul wrapped around his smallest claw. Let's ask him to lead the way to Wilhelm. But, I must warn you—when he gets cranky, he can be difficult. And Wilhelm is often cranky."

Arcturus agreed to lead us to the Royal Spook, as he called him. He telepathed that the ghost found the name pleasing, but only when used by his close friends. "Could count his mates on one paw, I could, with toes left over," he explained. "But, no need to go at it full lick, could be a clever rat's age before His Royal Spookness lets you breathe that rarified air."

And off he went, white spots flashing, as though there were strobe lights on his pedals to ward off traffic. The cat knew it could outrace us, and so waited at every turn, keeping us in sight. We all hurried. El was well ahead of Nandia and me. The ageless chambermaid moved as if she trained daily with Arcturus.

As we scurried through the halls, I recalled an earlier curiosity and mentally asked, "El, how long have you been working for the royal family?"

Her laughter bounced off the walls ahead of us. "Dear Bearns, I was Sabre's great, great-grandfather's third wife—that is, until he died," she explained. "And, that was over three hundred years ago. But he wasn't my first husband." It suddenly occurred to me that we were in the presence of an immortal queen. My newly heightened respect for this woman was quite humbling. Especially knowing that, now, she was serving as a royal chambermaid and seemed quite happy doing so.

I began to wonder what I could bring to this mission that El didn't already have. But, then it hit me that the Council Elders had most likely chosen this team for the gestalt of our combined energies. I decided I could trust the Council and looked up from my musings. I'd had fallen behind the others and ran to catch up. Together we hurried up more stairways and down new hallways, always pushing ourselves to keep pace with the cat.

Arcturus finally guided us up a spiral staircase that led into a domed turret towering over the surrounding structures. From its apex hung a massive bell, its pull shredded and decaying after decades of neglect. I wondered how long it had been since anyone had actually heard that bell peal.

The cat leapt up onto a wooden bench built along the tower's circular walls. There, he sniffed out a suitable spot for a nap. As he was settling in, he deigned to notice us and mentally telepathed, "Linger together. Better with oglers flapped. Let yourselves tingle the ghost's shroud." It was only when I saw El close her eyes that I had any idea of what the cat was talking about.

So, finally we had a chance to rest. It took a few moments for me catch my breath and then I remembered to take deep, connected breaths. I began relaxing, releasing tensions that had accumulated since our arrival in Sabre's ballroom.

As I calmed down, I recalled a question I'd been longing to ask Nandia—similar to the one I'd so recently asked of El. During our time in Geasa, I found myself wondering if Nandia had been traveling much longer than the appearance of her tender years had led me to believe. But, the priorities of our mission dissuaded me the several times I was about to ask. I decided that now was the time to yield to my curiosity ...

But, she had been eavesdropping again, the snoop. Her soothing voice interrupted as she telepathed, "Not yet, Bearns, not quite yet ..."

AFTERWORDS

ALL THE HEALING ABILITIES AND MODALITIES used in *Nandia's Copper* are within the reach of human endeavor today. In truth, each of us heals in our own unique ways, and each act of healing is, in itself, its own unique creation.

The mention, within these pages, of an organization made up of alternative healers who discovered a remedy for a wide range of emotional imbalances actually exists. You can learn more about them at www.HealersWhoShare.com.

The names of people and locales in The Nandia Trilogy were all chosen for their specific meaning to the tale of which each is a part. While I have attempted to replicate certain characters' dialects as faithfully as possible, any failures in the accuracy of idioms and cultural expressions are mine, and mine alone. For those, I apologize.

My heartfelt thanks go out to the many beloved friends, family and supporters who have made the publication of The Nandia Trilogy possible. Especially to Mary-Ann, your joy and encouragement have been an ongoing inspiration. Hajo, your editing wisdom has long served to strengthen my skills and vastly improve the final result. Wendy, your artistic creativity has given Nandia an eternal beauty. And, my heartfelt gratitude goes to to sister Margaret, as well as Jerry, Joanna, Renee and the many others who offered welcome encouragement through the many renditions of Nandia's Copper. To Erik, Carol and the rest of the fine folks at Longfeather Book Design, I trust your patience and dedicated hard work have been fully recognized.

To all of you, may you know this is only one of many expressions of my deepest gratitude. Together, we have brought Nandia to life. And, she will travel these many worlds of adventure again.

CPSIA information can be obtained
at www.ICGtesting.com
Printed in the USA
FSHW04n0928260318
46172FS

9 780967 557540